# CT
# ESCAPE

DANIEL HURST

www.danielhurstbooks.com

# Download My Free Book

*If you would like to receive a FREE copy of my psychological thriller 'Just One Second', then you can find the link to the book at my website www.danielhurstbooks.com*

# PROLOGUE

The first thing that the male dog walker who occasionally wandered through these parts of the woods noticed was that the impressive barn was now gone.

The barn had been situated at the bottom of a very large garden, and while he didn't know for sure because he had never spoken to the owners, he had always suspected the barn was used as a type of holiday home, a place a person could rent when they needed a brief respite from life.

Stepping through the treeline and into the edge of the garden, the dog walker stroked his chin as he wondered why the owners here would get rid of such a beautiful and potentially lucrative building like that. Looking around the sprawling garden, he couldn't see those owners around because if he did, he would surely have asked them where the barn went. But all he could see was the house at the top of the garden, the large stone cottage that was almost as pretty as the barn had been.

Shrugging his shoulders, the man was content enough to turn back and carry on along the trail that cut through these woods in the Kent countryside. But just before he could be on his way, his dog, a very energetic border terrier, shot off in the direction of the house, and despite his best efforts, his owner lost his grip on the leash and watched his pet race away.

'Freddie! Come back!'

But Freddie didn't listen, and while he had no idea what had got his canine so worked up, he had no choice but to chase after him to get him back.

As he continued to call out his dog's name, the man made his way through the garden, past where the barn used to stand and up towards the house. When he got there, he saw the front door was wide open, and Freddie was nowhere to be seen.

*He must have gone inside.*

Fearful that the dog might just be about to get him in a lot of trouble, the man called out to find out if there was anybody inside. But he got no answer, so he had no one to apologise to yet. Feeling a little anxious, the man stepped through the open doorway and entered the house, praying that his pet wasn't destroying any of the furniture or attacking any other pets that may reside here. But when he saw his beloved dog, he could never have imagined what he was actually doing.

*He was licking the face of a dead body.*

Putting a hand to his mouth in shock, the man stared at the female corpse on the floor and noticed a couple of things. One, the deceased had been an attractive woman in her mid-forties with long black hair and a fashionable sense of style. And two, there was rather a large pool of blood surrounding the back of her head, the result of a blow or possible bullet wound she had suffered to the skull.

This was clearly a crime scene, and the police needed to be called immediately, so the man reached into his pocket to grab his mobile phone. But there was no signal, and he shook his head because he should have already known that. This area was notorious for being a difficult place to make a phone call from, and while some liked how it was possible to come to places like this and be uncontactable, it wasn't helping this dog walker much now.

Fortunately, his phone had the capability for him to make an emergency call even without a signal, so he used that option. As he prepared to speak to the operator, he tried to get his dog away from the body because it was hardly respectful to have Freddie licking her.

This woman deserved to rest in peace, whoever she was.

But how had she died?

Had somebody come here and murdered her?

If so, who?

And while that was the main mystery the police would have to solve, the dog walker was still keen to solve the other mystery about this place.

Where had that barn gone at the bottom of the garden?

Did that have something to do with what had happened to this woman?

Who was the last person to stay there?

*And were they the killer?*

# *BEFORE*

# 1

## FAY

We just needed a place to get away from it all. That was the reason why I decided to book a night's stay at the converted barn house in the Kent Downs, a part of England designated as an area of Outstanding Natural Beauty and a part of the country that plenty of other people have enjoyed a quiet getaway in over the years.

I've never been so far down south before, spending all my thirty-nine years of life well north of Birmingham, excluding several trips abroad to sunnier climes. But I've well and truly hit the road today, as has my husband, Aidan, as we've made our way along the motorway from Yorkshire, navigated a few of the chaotic roads leading in and out of London and eventually, made it into the county nicknamed 'The Garden of England'.

Such an illustrious title conjures up images of colourful flowers and rolling green hills, and that's mainly what I've seen through my passenger window as our car has moved through this area. There were plenty of pretty towns on the way that the pair of us could have stopped at for a snack and a chance to stretch our legs, but we kept going, and now we are very close to our final destination, which is the barn house we have rented for tonight for what could be considered quite an extortionate price. Then again, you get what you pay for, and we are more than happy to pay a little extra to get the kind of accommodation that suits our fairly demanding needs.

This trip has been undertaken as more of a necessity than a random splurge, borne of a desire for my partner and me to get away before things got too much and life consumed us. But doesn't everybody feel like that from time to time? Overwhelmed. Exhausted. Desperate for a change of scene and eager to disconnect from the real world for a limited amount of time.

Aidan and I certainly felt that way, which is why I made this booking, and I'm glad I did because I feel better already, and we're not even there yet.

We're currently about twenty miles away from the barn house, having stopped at a service station to refuel and have a comfort break. Aidan has filled up the tank with petrol, and we've both visited the bathrooms here, but I'm the only one who is ready to get on the road again. My husband is still inside the service station because, much to my chagrin, he decided to go into one of the shops inside and buy snacks.

I told him we didn't need them, but would he listen? Apparently, he has gone as far as he can on this journey before he needs to load up with calorific crisps and chocolate, and I'm sure that whatever he brings back to this car will work wonders in adding a few inches to his ever-expanding waistline. But the food will most likely do the same to my waistline, too, because even though I don't want anything to eat, I know I'll be unable to resist tucking into something when Aidan is back in the car and gorging himself in the driver's seat beside me.

Keeping a lookout for him, I see several people exit the service station and make their way to their vehicles, but my husband is not among them. I have no idea what is taking him so long in there, but there's not much I can do to speed him up, so I'll just have to wait. At least we do have a little time to spare because we're not allowed into the barn house for another half an hour.

I'm glad that I opted for the early check-in because otherwise, we would have had to wait until 3 pm to go inside. But by selecting the midday option, it means it won't be long until we're inside the barn house with our feet up and a very quiet afternoon and evening ahead of us, which is just what we both need.

Aidan and I have worked too much recently, and we have both reached the point of burnout, that deceptively dangerous state of exhaustion caused by spending far too long a period being subjected to mental and physical stress. We run a business together, and while it seemed like a good idea at the time we started it, little did we know just how much it was going to take out of the two of us. What started out as a seemingly good idea quickly descended into far too much time spent dealing with finances, clients and paperwork, and while it crept up on us, it reached the point when we both realised we couldn't carry on as we were. Something had to change, and that something has led us here, to the Kent countryside, not too far from the white cliffs of Dover, a sight I might catch a glimpse of during our time in this part of the world.

Booking a night at the barn house that comes recommended by friends and has such good reviews has been long overdue, but now it's finally happening. But it's not only the comfortable interior of the barn or the idyllic setting it is placed in that has us looking forward to being there so much. It's also the fact that it is known as one of those places that are 'technology free'. That means there are no electronic devices in the property, making it impossible to be in contact with the outside world or be contacted by anybody else in it.

No phone calls. No emails. No text messages.
No internet. No television. No mobile phone signal.
Complete and utter quiet.
Fully off the grid.

*Proper peace.*

Such a thing was important to us. Truth be told, it was a non-negotiable rather than an added extra. The only way Aidan and I will be able to enjoy ourselves is if we can't be reached by anybody else, nor find ourselves picking up our mobiles and looking for something to occupy our tired minds with on there.

The main reason a night at the barn house is so expensive is because of how much effort has gone into making it a place where guests can truly unwind, and the couple who own the property certainly struck gold when they had the idea, that's for sure. It's not easy to reserve a stay, but we're about to join the lucky few who have managed to get in, and soon, we'll be experiencing all the barn house has to offer.

'Come on, what are you doing?' I say under my breath as I continue to wait for Aidan to emerge from inside the service station. He's taking an awfully long time, but there might just be a big queue at the checkout, and there's always somebody who slows everybody else down by taking an age to pay for their goods. I'm sure

he'll be out any second now, appearing with a shopping bag in hand and a big smile on his face.
That's one thing I envy about my husband: his boundless positivity. He can find something to be happy about in the worst of situations, whereas I've always been more the kind of person who constantly worries. Sometimes, I am more than entitled to be worried, but I'm the same even if things are going well because in those moments, I'm wondering how long it will last until things go wrong again. But Aidan has a relaxed, optimistic way about him, believing things will always work out well in the end, and as I suddenly spot him walking out behind a rotund man in an unflattering green overcoat, I am right with my prediction.
*He does have a shopping bag in his hand and a big smile on his face.*

I would laugh at his silly grin if I wasn't so irritated at him for taking ages in the service station and making this long journey last even longer than it should, but that would only encourage him, and he certainly doesn't need any more encouragement. He knows he's a handsome guy and that, mixed with his chirpy demeanour, has meant that he has gone through most of his life with other people not only liking him, but doing whatever he says. But while he did admittedly charm me when we first met, I've built up somewhat of an immunity to his personality and looks, admiring them when I want to but also having the choice to not be swayed when I choose not to be. Maybe that's why it's me sitting in this car now with the wedding ring on my finger rather than any of the other women he was with in his past. He can't control me as well as his exes. I give as good as I get, and I challenge him as much as he challenges me. At least, that's what I like to think anyway. Then again, maybe I'm the one he ultimately chose to be with forever because I looked good in a minidress and turned his head the night he met me as I breezed past him in a blur of blonde hair, white teeth and red lipstick.

However, one thing is for sure as I observe Aidan crossing the car park towards me.

*I no longer look anything like I did that night we met five years ago.*

Part of that is simply down to the passage of time and the ways it changes a body the more months and years accumulate, but it's also down to me recently choosing to go through somewhat of a transformation. I've changed my hair colour and am now a redhead, a colour Aidan was not completely enamoured with at first, though he assures me it is now growing on him, and he will get used to it.

I know I'm not the first person to approach forty and have something of a makeover, but I've never claimed to be original. I'm not alone in tinkering with my appearance because plenty of others do it too, my husband included. Where he was once clean-shaven, he is now going for the more rugged look, and it's alarming how quickly his facial hair grows when he doesn't trim it. I suspect he'll have a full beard in a week or so, and then he really will look different to how he looked on our wedding day.

I wasn't a fan at first, but I have to admit he quite suits a bit of stubble, although I do wish he wouldn't sit there stroking his chin so much now, acting as if he is some wise old wizard just because there is hair on the bottom half of his head as well as on the top. But funnily enough, while his facial hair has become more prominent, the hair on top of his head is less so thanks to the baseball cap he has taken to wearing recently. The cap has a big red 'B' on the front of it, which apparently represents the Boston Red Sox baseball team, though quite why my partner picked that one is beyond me because he has never been to Boston before, nor has he watched a single minute of any baseball game with them or any other team playing in it. But that's not stopping him from wearing it proudly as he opens the driver side door and gets in next to me.

'What took you so long?' I ask him as he closes the door again.

'It's busy in there,' Aidan replies with a shrug before pulling a chocolate bar out of the shopping bag and offering it to me.

'No, thanks,' I say, putting on my seatbelt to show him that I'm ready to get going again. But Aidan is still in no rush, his carefree, almost child-like persona on display yet again as he tears the wrapper and scoffs the chocolate before opening the bag again and looking for something else.

'You're going to get fat,' I warn Aidan, not that he'll be bothered about such a thing.

'And I'm going to be happy doing it,' he replies with a wink before opening another chocolate bar.

As I feared it would, my willpower only lasts for so long, and before I know it, I am consuming chocolate too, not doing much to get Aidan to speed up and put this car in motion again. But when I'm finished, I tell him to get a move on, and he thankfully listens to me, starting the engine and steering us out of this car park before we get back onto the country road that will lead us to the barn house.

We're due to be there in twenty minutes, so I hope the place is ready for us, though I'm sure it will be. That's because the barn house is not the only thing that has come recommended.

The owner of it has too.

# 2

## BRIDGETTE

As any good host should, I always take it seriously whenever I have new guests coming to stay. But I take it even more seriously whenever a guest requests early check-in because that tells me that they are keen to begin their stay as early as possible and have no qualms about paying the extra price that comes with that.
Wanting to arrive three hours earlier suggests they are super eager to gain access to the barn house and if that's the case, then I am never going to stand in their way, and not just because I appreciate the extra cash. It's because I know how hard it can be for a person who needs a break from life, so I intend to make things as easy as possible for them.

That is just one of the many reasons why I and my rental property come so highly recommended.

I'm in the barn house now putting the finishing touches on how it looks before the next guests arrive, and at this point, all the big tasks are already done. The bedding has been washed and re-laid; all the carpets have been hoovered and the surfaces dusted, and the washing up has been done, ensuring everything is as clean as it can be, and cleanliness is always a big priority for any guest. But while this place is looking respectable, and I know I could get away with just letting the beauty of the property do much of the impressing for me, I always go a few extra yards to add some final touches.

Like the bottle of champagne that I place in the ice bucket beside two glasses, sitting in the middle of the dining room table next to a box of chocolates. Or like the map I leave by the side of the double bed, the one that shows the guests how to get around the local area, including the most direct route to the coast, because that's always a helpful thing for any visitor who is unfamiliar with their new surroundings. And like the handwritten note I write for every guest who stays here, the one that says I am contactable at all times and a guest should never hesitate to ask for anything if they need something during their stay.

I love being a host and because I enjoy it, I'm good at it. That means the money keeps rolling in and the more it does, the more it proves me right and my partner wrong.

Logan, my husband of four years and the man who helped pay for the majority of the building work that converted this old barn into a place worthy of having people staying in it, was not easily sold on the idea of us having a rental property when I first suggested it. He thought it would be an awful lot of work for very little money and was happy to just keep things as they were, which mainly consisted of him earning money from his day job while I sat around our house and did very little. But I have always prided myself on having an eye to spot opportunities, and that was why I had pestered my husband until he had eventually given in and agreed to allow me to start my own little business on our land.

We moved into our house, a three-bedroom cottage in the middle of nowhere, not long after we married, and I enjoyed the very remote and very quiet life for a while. It was fun in the beginning not to have to worry about work and money and just enjoy waking up every day without any stress. But still, only being in my forties meant I knew I couldn't just do that forever, and I longed for a challenge, a project to sink my teeth into and dare I say it, a little excitement, and I knew I would get that whenever I made the short walk down the gravel driveway from the cottage to the dilapidated old barn that sat at the bottom of our expansive back garden.

The barn came with the cottage simply because it was already on the land, but all we really got at the time of purchase was an eyesore of a thing that Logan and I spent very little time around. Logan was quite happy to just leave the barn to fall into further ruin because he hardly ever went that far down into our garden to be around it much, so it was out of sight and out of mind as far as he was concerned. But I had started to find myself taking regular walks down to the barn to have a closer look at it, and while I hadn't dared go inside in case something fell on my head, I had stood outside it and spent an awful lot of time imagining what the building could be if it just had a little TLC.

It's amazing how a little affectionate attention can do so much to something previously unloved.

*And it sure did that to this barn house.*

As I continue to move around the barn and make sure it really is ready for its guests, I smile to myself, as I often do when I am here, at just how much of a transformation this building has undergone.

Gone are the rotting beams, broken windows and the very sizeable hole in the roof. The entire frame of the barn was rebuilt from the finest timber; the windows have been triple-glazed, and now the only hole in the roof comes in the form of a skylight in the kitchen that helps to flood that wonderfully fitted room with some extra daylight. As well as that, there are plush carpets throughout the entire place, adding warmth to this barn, not that it needs it with the large fireplace in here too. To add comfort and entertainment, there are large sofas in the lounge, a waterfall shower in the decadent bathroom and a bookcase stocked with all sorts of fascinating autobiographies written by people who, to me, are some of the most interesting people who have ever lived. I'm talking entrepreneurs, A-List celebrities and even a few notorious criminals, and while they might not have been the most savoury of characters, they sure do have an interesting tale to tell.

However, it's not so much what this place is made up of that is important but, rather, what it lacks, and that is something very important to both me and my guests.

*A connection to the outside world.*

I told Logan very early on that I didn't just want to rebuild the barn house so it could be a place that generated mostly passive income for us but that I wanted it to be a place where those who stayed here could truly get the peace and privacy that everybody deserves at some time in their life. Advertising this as a place that offered guests a full retreat from the chaos of modern life gave it a unique selling point. There are plenty of rentals where people can go and watch TV, browse the internet and be contactable at all times. But there aren't many that make those things impossible, though this barn house is one of them.

After a final sweep of the barn to make sure it truly is ready, I check my watch and see that the guests should be here in the next ten minutes. That gives me just enough time to leave this place and walk back to the cottage and go and check on the cake that is currently baking in the oven. While Logan will welcome our guests as soon as he sees their car arrive, I will stay out of sight until the cake is ready and only appear once it is. I'll do that by coming back down here to hand deliver the cake to the guests myself before wishing them a lovely stay. I know the cake isn't necessary, but I see it as a nice touch, and I'm sure my guests will too.

Leaving the barn and locking the door, I stride up the gravel driveway towards my cottage, feeling pleased at the prospect of another successful and lucrative rental of the property I'm leaving. While my husband had a few concerns at the beginning of this project, he has far less now that he has seen how much money it can generate for us - money that we can then use on nice things for ourselves. But it's not all been plain sailing, I have to admit, and as my boots crunch on the gravel beneath me, I think about the guests who stayed with us three months ago, the ones who ended up trashing the place after drinking too much alcohol and getting carried away with their 'holiday.' But while it was a shock to see red wine stains on the carpet, a hole in one of the sofa cushions and a broken mirror in the bedroom, I made sure I did not end up out of pocket for the repair costs. All it took was me threatening to call the police, and the guests quickly apologised and offered to pay for the cost to repair the damage, proving that while they were certainly reckless with my property, they did not wish to be so reckless with the law.

Logan saw what happened as a sign that we should perhaps curtail the barn house business, reminding me that we didn't need the money or the hassle it generated, but I was not having any of it. I love the barn and love what it offers to other people. It would be selfish if we just kept it for ourselves. We should share it with others, namely those who are in desperate need of a night or two in its calming bosom, and that is why it remains fully open for business.

I make it back to the cottage and go inside before there is any sign of a car arriving on these premises, which is just the way I wanted it, and as I re-enter my home, I smell the cake in the oven. The fragrant scent coming from the kitchen is a promising one and suggests that the baking part of the process has gone well, and when I open the oven and take a quick peek inside, I get confirmation of that.

It looks great, smells great and I'm sure it is going to taste great too.

Figuring that it just needs a couple more minutes until I can take it from the oven and leave it to cool on the countertop, I check my watch and see that it has just gone twelve. Right on cue, I hear the sound of tyres on gravel and glance out of my kitchen window to see a car trundling towards the cottage.

'They're here!' I call out to Logan and no sooner have I done that than I hear footsteps above my head telling me that my partner is mobile now and is on his way down to greet our guests.

This is a well-worked routine that Logan and I run through, a system that ensures both of us are visible and receptive to our guests when they get here, which undoubtedly helps put them at ease and removes any doubts they might have about having booked to stay here. I'm aware that it might be a slight issue for some guests that the barn house is technically part of our garden and that the cottage is close, meaning that a guest might feel it could be a little awkward to be in fairly close proximity to the hosts. That's why I go the extra mile to remove any of that awkwardness as early as possible, and as Logan goes outside to meet the arriving car, I turn off the oven and take the cake out.

As the cake cools and the scent of it takes a further stranglehold over this house, I smile to myself but not just because everything has gone to plan. I am smiling because I know there is somebody else who will be able to smell this delicious cake now, and it will be driving her mad that she won't be getting her hands on it.

*That would be the woman I currently have locked up in the basement of this cottage.*

Nobody knows she is down there but me. My husband has no idea because the basement door is always locked and as far as he is concerned, we don't need a key for it because there's no reason that we'd ever need to use that room anyway. But I have the key, and I use that room all the time.

*I use it to hold my prisoner.*

I keep smiling as I watch Logan wave to the couple arriving outside and think about how our guests would react if they found out what I was hiding too.

I imagine they would turn and run if they knew my secret.

But they don't know it, so that is why they are now parking up and getting out of their car to begin their stay.

# 3

## FAY

We've finally made it to the barn house, and it's a huge relief to be here. After many hours of travelling, a stop at a service station that was longer than anticipated, and one wrong turn at the last minute that we thankfully corrected before we wasted too much time, we are now here to check in and begin our stay.

I haven't seen the barn yet, but I have seen the cottage where the hosts live, and it is a beautiful property.

*But it's the location that is really enviable.*

After turning off the country lane and entering onto a winding track that cut through a small wooded area, it was obvious that this place was exactly as advertised.

*Off the grid.*

It's funny, but the further we drove down that track, the more relaxed I became, and by the time we turned onto the gravel driveway that runs past the cottage, I was so glad I had found out about this place and booked to come.

Things look even more promising when I see a man coming out to greet us as we park - a handsome-looking guy in his mid-forties with toned arms, slick black hair and the kind of smile that could make me blush if only I wasn't already taken. I dealt with his partner when it came to booking our stay here, but there is no sign of her yet, though I'm sure she's around somewhere.

From what I've heard, the hosts here only venture out when they buy groceries and are otherwise always here, enjoying the peace and privacy that their hard work has earnt them, and who can blame them? If I lived here permanently, then I would hardly leave either.

'Hello. Welcome,' the man says as he holds out his hand towards Aidan. 'I'm Logan. Nice to meet you. I hope you found us okay?'

I watch as Logan shakes hands with my husband, who is quick to reply that we had no trouble getting here, but my partner is the kind who would say that even if we had because he wouldn't want to bring the mood down. Logan is pleased to hear it before he turns his attention to me, and I make sure to smile before offering my hand too.

'Hi, I'm Fay. Nice to meet you,' I say as we shake, and as I'm closer to him now, I see that Logan also has a pair of nice eyes to go with his cool name.

'Thanks for booking to stay with us here. I guess you guys are eager to get to the barn, so let's get you checked in, and then I'll leave you to enjoy it,' Logan says breezily, no doubt so casual because he has said the same thing to all the other people who have booked here ahead of us, and this is just all part of the routine for him.

'I'll walk down to the barn. You can follow me in your car,' Logan tells us, gesturing further along the driveway, though when I look, I can't see the barn yet, just a large garden flanked on all sides by tall trees.

'Sure. No problem,' Aidan replies before hopping back in behind the wheel, and I get back into the car, too, before we restart the engine and slowly start following Logan down the driveway.

The road dips as we get further away from the cottage and when it does, we are treated to a quite magnificent view of a wooded area in the distance. But it's what is standing in front of the woods that really captivates me.

I get my first look at the barn in the flesh.

*And it's beautiful.*

'Now we're talking,' Aidan says with a grin, proving that the barn has impressed him too and made this long journey to get here worth it. We haven't even seen the inside yet, but we're both already sold on it as we continue to slowly drive behind Logan, who is marching towards the barn with all the pride of the person who owns this magnificent structure.

I feel the tension leaving my shoulders as we get closer, further and further from the country lane we came here on and deeper into this huge, lush and green back garden. This is the kind of garden I thought I'd have one day, a big one for a couple of kids to run around in, and while that might still happen, it's a long way off yet. But I shouldn't dwell on that because I came here to forget about my worries for a night, and as Logan points to a spot on the driveway he wishes for us to park in, we are now finally about to begin this break.

'Wow, this is some place you have here,' Aidan says after he has turned off the engine and got out of the car again. 'If you don't mind me asking, how much did it cost you to build this barn?'

I cringe at my husband's question, well aware of how money-orientated he can be and how that leads him to always ask things of other people that should be considered private information. I've lost count of how many times Aidan has asked somebody how much they earn or how much their car cost, but that's just him; he loves to earn money and has never been shy in asking others about the fruits of their labour. Fortunately, Logan doesn't seem shy in having a conversation like this one and has an answer for my curious spouse.

'The whole project cost almost eighty thousand pounds,' Logan replies, and Aidan whistles when he hears that figure.

'Wow, that's a big investment, although I guess it was worth it for you once the rental money started rolling in,' Aidan says, and Logan agrees that it has.

'It could have all been done a little cheaper, I suppose,' Logan says. 'But the old barn was so dilapidated that we had to completely tear it down. Then my wife wanted all the finest materials, so that bumped the cost up quite significantly.'

'Ahh, so you have a partner who likes to spend money like it's going out of fashion just like I do,' Aidan says before looking at me.

'Hey, I'm not that bad!' I say in my defence, but Aidan knows the truth. I guess I do like to spend money on the finer things in life if I can afford it, but who doesn't? It's fun, and that's what life should be about, isn't it? Besides, I'm not half as bad as my husband is when it comes to that. While I spend what I have, Aidan likes to spend what he thinks he will have in the future, and there is a very big difference there.

'Do you need a hand with your luggage?' Logan asks us as we take out our suitcases, but we tell him that we can manage and thank him before he goes to unlock the barn.

'Right, let's get you inside, and I'll run through a couple of things about your stay here, and then I can leave you to it,' the host says as he opens the barn door and welcomes us in.

I go ahead of Aidan and enter the barn first, and once I'm in and have put down my heavy suitcase, I take in the luxurious interior.

'Wow, this place is wonderful,' I say as I admire everything from the carpet to the curtains to the champagne bottle on the table, which I presume is for us.

'There's a thermostat here if you need to put the heating on,' Logan says as he points to a small device fixed to the wall behind one of the sofas. 'Or you can start a fire if you'd like. There's plenty of wood in the box there, but if you need me to get it going for you, just give me a shout.'

'That's okay, I think I can manage with that,' Aidan says, and I knew he would because he wouldn't want to admit to not being able to get a fire going himself and risk being emasculated, not that I care about things like that.

'The kitchen is through here,' Logan goes on, walking through a wide doorway, and we follow him into a small but tastefully decorated room where I see Logan open the fridge and tell us that he has stocked us up with a few basics like milk, cheese and a couple of beers he thought Aidan might like.

'You're a Yorkshireman, right?' Logan says as he holds up one of the bottles of the beer that is brewed in Leeds, which isn't far from us at all, and Aidan is very pleased with the personal touch.

'There's a small utility room through here if you need to do any washing,' Logan goes on, opening a door at the back of the kitchen and showing us a washing machine, not that I plan to use that while I'm here. 'Other than that, there's the bedroom and bathroom upstairs and that's it, so you shouldn't get too lost in here.'

Logan chuckles at his own joke, but Aidan and I make sure to find it amusing too, before we leave the kitchen and head back through the open-plan lounge/dining area.

'Can I help take your cases up to your bedroom?' Logan asks, but I tell him we are fine, which Aidan rolls his eyes at because he'll be the one who has to carry them up there anyway, rather than me.

'Okay, well, that's it from me. I'll leave you in peace, but my wife will be down shortly. She has a little surprise for you. Don't worry, it's nothing weird, just a little something she has prepared for your arrival.'

'You don't need to do that,' I say. 'This is already perfect.'

'It's no trouble,' Logan tells me with a friendly smile before he steps outside the barn. 'I'm sure I'll see you again, but enjoy your stay and remember, if you need anything, just come and ask.'

'Cheers, mate,' Aidan says, and he goes to close the door but just before he can, Logan clears his throat and looks at us a little awkwardly.

'Erm, sorry, I don't suppose you would be able to pay for your stay now?' he asks sheepishly.

That's when I remember we haven't actually settled our bill here, and feeling foolish for accepting this man's warm welcome without remembering to pay him for letting us stay on his land, I nudge Aidan and ask him to get the money.

'Of yes, of course. Sorry about that,' Aidan says, though I wonder if he forgot as I did or was just hoping we could get away with not paying, which would be incredibly cheeky as well as incredibly unlikely.

'There you go,' Aidan says as he hands Logan the appropriate funds and Logan thanks us before heading away, and I thank him myself before closing the door behind him.

'He's a nice guy, isn't he?' Aidan says chirpily as he goes to inspect the woodpile.

'Really nice,' I agree as my attention turns to the gift that has been left for us on the table.

'How about a drink?' I say as I approach the champagne, and Aidan says that sounds like a good plan, and he will join me in a moment once he has taken the suitcases up to the bedroom.

As he goes upstairs, I plan to pop the cork on this bottle and fill up the glasses with the cool, fizzy bubbles but just before I do that, I notice there is a small note sitting beside the champagne bucket, so I pick it up to see what's written on it.

***Enjoy your getaway.***

'I'll drink to that,' I say as I put the card down and pick up the champagne bottle. As I open the cork and hear Aidan let out an excited cheer from upstairs, I smile because so far, this is perfect.

Our hosts get it.

They knew what we needed, and they are giving it to us.

I've already thanked Logan, but I will thank his wife when she comes to see us shortly.

He said she'd be here any minute.

Until then, I'll have a sip of champers and unwind.

# 4

## BRIDGETTE

The cake I have made for our guests is still cooling on the kitchen counter, but I'm busy preparing another item of food at the moment. However, unlike the cake, I'm not putting anywhere near as much love and attention into the making of this particular meal, and as I cut the plain cheese sandwich in half, I stare at it on the plate and amuse myself over what a pathetically inadequate meal it is.

A sandwich like this will do for somebody as a snack, no doubt, but that's on the assumption they will get a much heartier and healthier meal at some other point of the day. But this meal on the plate in front of me that consists of four-day-old bread and a dried-out slice of cheddar is barely fit for human consumption as it is, never mind it being the only thing that the person who eats it will be getting today to satisfy their hunger.

Looking out the window to make sure Logan is not coming back yet, I see no sign of him and expect he is still running our new guests through a few of the facilities at the barn. That's perfect because while he's down at the bottom of our big garden doing that, I am free to be up here in the house doing what I need to get done in private.

Carrying the plate with the pathetic cheese sandwich on it, I make my way through our warm, cosy cottage to the door in the centre of the property, a door that is always locked and only opens when I put the key into it. As I take out that key and slide it into the lock, I think about what my husband would say if he knew I had this. As far as he is concerned, this door and the basement beyond it is a useless part of the cottage, a place neither of us can go or want to go. But as I turn the key and hear a loud click, I think that this part of our home is fast becoming my favourite part of the house.

As I pull open the very old and very creaky door and look inside, I see nothing but darkness, but that is not unusual. It's always that way in the basement until I turn the light on, which is helpful should anybody ever somehow manage to open this door and peek inside. They'd see nothing but inky black if they did, and that should put them off going in any further, especially because they wouldn't know where the light switch was. But I know where it is, and as I reach up and find the small switch on the wall that's just behind a black curtain that hangs down over it to make it extra hidden, I prepare to flood this basement with light.

One flick of the switch and now I can see where I am going, and as I look down the staircase in front of me, I count the nine steps that will take me down to where I need to be. From here, even with the light on, a person couldn't see much to alarm them. It's only if they descended a little deeper that they would start to realise that this basement harboured something very unusual, something it shouldn't be harbouring, and I know that it will come into view when I get down to the fifth step.

One step, two steps, three steps, four. My heart rate increases as I put my feet on each one until I make it to the fifth before I stop and smile.

'Hello, Holly,' I say calmly as I stare at the woman tied by rope to the rail on the stone wall.

But Holly doesn't offer anything back, staying quiet, though it hasn't always been this way. Naturally, she spent some time crying out for help when I first put her down here, though it was all in vain. I know any sounds made in here do not carry all the way upstairs to the main house from my own experience calling out to my husband when we moved in here. Despite shouting his name as loud as I could, he never heard me, allowing me to realise this place is effectively soundproof, though I did have to conduct a test to be sure. Logan wouldn't be the first man in the world to ignore the call of his wife so I had him stand in the basement and shout out to me, but sure enough, I didn't hear anything upstairs either.

Little did I know how convenient such a thing would come to be.

'I've brought you something to eat,' I say as I walk down the last few steps before approaching my increasingly timid and tired prisoner. For the first few days she was down here, Holly would be wriggling and writhing when she saw me, desperate to break free from her restraints and either get out of here or get at me. But it's been just over a week now since I first put her down here, and as time has gone on, she has become more placid. I guess she has slowly but surely learnt to accept her fate and has realised that no amount of defiance is going to make a difference to her predicament.

She'll only get out of here if I let her.

*But why would I want to do a thing like that?*

'I hope you're hungry,' I say with a smirk as I place the plate down on the ground near enough for her to reach out and take it but not too close that she could take a swipe at me first. While Holly is tied to the wall, there is enough slack in her restraint to enable her to both sit and stand, as well as take a few steps in either direction. That is good because it allows her to not only get a tiny bit of exercise but also visit the small potty I leave out for her, the one in which she does her daily business, not that she needs to use it too much because I don't exactly keep her well fed and watered. I just provide her with enough sustenance to stay alive, nothing more, because anything more would be a waste.

I don't need her to be healthy; I just need her alive long enough to think about what she has done. But she's had long enough to do that now, so soon, this will all be over.

*She just doesn't know it yet.*

But for now, I have to keep my prisoner going, so along with the sandwich I have just brought her, I check on her water levels. I can get those from seeing how much liquid is left in the large water bottle that sits on the ground next to her and it's only a quarter full, telling me Holly is rather sensibly rationing it. That's because she's learnt by now that I do not make a habit of keeping that bottle topped up. I figure that will be enough liquid to keep her going until I come and see her again tomorrow. For now, I will just clear out her potty, so I pick it up and take it out of the basement, working quickly because Logan will be back very soon.

Once that tedious task has been completed, I return to the basement and place the fresh potty back down, not too far from where the cheese sandwich still sits on the plate.

'What's the matter? You wanted something else?' I say with a chuckle. 'Too bad. That's all you're getting today, so I'd eat up if I was you. Get some strength. Or just wither away and die. Your choice. But I will say this. You would be making my life a lot easier if you did just give up and die. That way, it would save me from having to figure out what to do with you next.'

I watch Holly's face to gauge her reaction, and even though she is weak and exhausted, I see a flicker of a response behind her eyes, no doubt alarmed at me mentioning that she would be doing me a favour if she just stopped eating and drinking and faded away into oblivion. That's because so far, I have only told her why she is down here but not what will happen to her next. She knows it is the past that has seen her end up here, but she has no idea what her future holds.

I think about staying a minute longer and saying a few more things to Holly, and I have a few options. For example, I could goad her to get more of a reaction out of her. I could also revel in my victory over her and make myself feel even better while simultaneously making her feel even worse. I could also lament her for her previous actions and educate her on how to be a better woman, the type who doesn't end up in a situation like this. But I've done all those things before, so I wouldn't be saying anything that Holly hasn't already heard. But then I think of something new I could say to her, and it's sure to elicit an interesting response from her when she hears this.

'This will all be over very, very soon,' I tell Holly with a confidence that will surely make her nervous. 'In fact, that sandwich may very well end up being your last meal, so take your time with it. Enjoy it. Appreciate it. The same goes for the water too. Savour every single gulp you take because soon, you won't be able to eat or drink or do anything at all. Goodbye, Holly.'

With that, I turn for the stairs, but as expected, Holly doesn't want me to go and leave our 'little chat' on such a troubling note, and I know that because not only does she stand up, but she finally has something to say.

'Wait! What do you mean?' she wants to know, her voice incredibly raspy, no doubt a result of her hoarse throat from dehydration and the after-effects of straining her vocals cords to no avail during the early part of her captivity. I was taking to stuffing a handkerchief in her mouth when I first put her down here, just to be safe, but I've been using that less and less recently, though I keep it in my pocket just in case I feel the need to shut her up suddenly in the future.

I pause at the foot of the stairs and turn back to her and when I do, I see just how scared and helpless my prisoner really is. Her stomach is empty, and her eyes are full of fear, and as she continues to wriggle and make quiet, indiscernible sounds, I can't help but start laughing.

What started as a very crazy and possibly foolish plan has worked out quite well for me. I probably shouldn't have kidnapped this woman and brought her down here to be tied up and left to fight for her life, but now it's done, I'm glad I went to all the trouble. And it certainly has been trouble.

As I walk up the stairs, turn off the light and then lock the basement door behind me, I think about the effort this took for me to keep it all a secret from my husband. Having to get Holly here while he was out of the house was not easy. Have you any idea how hard it is to try and drag an unconscious woman into the basement of a cottage? It's tough work, but like any difficult manual task, it feels good once the effort has been exerted and the fruits of the labour can be admired.
I'm glad I did what I did, but I'm also able to appreciate that I can only do so much, which is why I just told Holly that this would be over soon.

It will.

*But will it be over in the way I want it to be?*

'They're all settled in at the barn,' Logan calls out to me a moment later as he re-enters the house. 'I told them you'd be down there with the cake shortly.'

'Thanks, love,' I say breezily. 'The cake's ready, so I'll go see them now.'

'Cool,' Logan says as he pours himself a glass of water and quenches his thirst, totally oblivious to what I have been doing while he was out of the house. But I'm not perfect, and just before I can walk out of the kitchen with the cake, he asks me why the bread is out.

Damn it, I forgot to finish clearing up after myself after I made that sandwich for Holly.

'Oh, that? I was just about to throw it away. It's going mouldy,' I say, and Logan grimaces before picking up what's left and tossing it in the food recycling bin.

'Urgh,' he says. 'Nothing worse than mouldy bread.'

I have to agree with him there.

And I'm sure Holly would agree, too, as she sits down there in the basement and eats her sandwich.

# 5

## AIDAN

Fay was right about this place. It is the perfect escape and is just what we both needed. We've only been here for ten minutes, but I'm already feeling much better about things - things that have been stressing me out and causing sleepless nights before now. I've had so much on my mind lately that it's been hard to keep my thoughts straight, but being in this barn house is helping greatly.

It's so quiet here, and for the first time in a long time, I have the peace to hear myself think.

People always assume my greatest trait is that I'm inherently positive and possess a carefree attitude, but I believe it is that I have the capacity to make long-term plans and see them through. The only problem is, it's hard to do that successfully when you're getting so much short-term grief, as I was before we got here. Work had gotten on top of me, and though I was partly to blame for letting it get to that point, it was hard to see any way out of the mess. But then Fay suggested we come here, and I have got to give it to my wife, she's made the right call.

'What do you think of the champagne?' she asks me as we sit beside each other on one of the sofas and sip the bubbles in our glasses.

'It's not bad,' I say. 'Especially as it was free.'

'I can't remember the last time we had champagne,' Fay mentions then, but I can.

'It was when we went to *San Diablos*,' I remind her, referring to a Spanish restaurant we have frequented often. 'Remember? When we took the team out to celebrate a successful quarter of profits.'

'Oh, yeah, that's right,' Fay says, remembering now, although I can see why it might have slipped her mind or seemed like a distant memory. That night at the classy restaurant in the heart of Leeds city centre was only just over a month ago, but a lot has happened since then. Little did we know it at the time but things were about to change for our business in a big way, and that was when the real stress started - stress that has resulted in us sitting in this barn and paying that lovely couple in the cottage for the privilege of being here for some respite.

Starting a business seemed like a great idea when I first had it. Not only would it finally give me the chance to be my own boss, which was something I had dreamed about ever since I first entered the working world as a fresh-faced sixteen-year-old, but it was an opportunity for Fay and me to work together. The demands of our previous jobs had meant that we spent most of the day apart, and even when we did see each other, we were both so exhausted that we did little more than grab a quick bite to eat and fall into bed to get some sleep before the next morning's commute. But I wanted there to be a way we could be around each other more, so when I had the idea for the business, I knew I wanted Fay by my side to help me run it.

It took a little convincing before my wife was on board with the idea, though, and I appreciated why. I was asking my partner to give up a safe and steady income at her previous job to launch a new business with me, one that had way more potential but carried no guarantees or assurances. Either it would be a success or it would fail, and we would have to go back to our old bosses and beg for our previous job back. But bless her, Fay eventually decided to take the plunge with me, and I saw that as a sure sign of how much she loved me that she was willing to help me chase a dream.

As I take another sip of champagne and decompress a little further, I reflect back on my business idea and how it really did seem like a good plan at the time. There are a few reasons for a person to decide to start their own company, but one of them is always money. The chance to get rich; who wouldn't want to try and do that? I was certainly eager to see if I could increase my annual income and figured that being my own boss would take off the ceiling on my earnings and make the potential limitless. That was why I started a social media marketing company, using skills I'd learned in my previous marketing roles to ride the wave of the fast-paced growth of the internet. But to make sure we stood the best chance of being up to date with the latest developments in the online world, I made sure to hire much younger employees, guys and girls in their twenties, who could focus on the social media side of things while my wife and I would manage the more 'adult tasks' like finance and administration.

Installing me and Fay as directors meant a lofty title each and the responsibility that came with it, but also ensured we'd be getting the bigger piece of the pie, and as things took off, it seemed like we'd made a great decision. The first two years were a dream, with the business growing month on month and the profits soaring, giving us both the kind of lifestyle that we had dreamt about as youngsters. What was just as special was being able to manage a team who were also benefiting greatly from the success of the business, and I was never shy to hand out bonuses to my staff, as well as treat them to regular work events in which all food and drink was free. I made sure we all worked hard but played hard and while that came with stress, it was never the kind that kept me up all night. But things ultimately changed for various reasons, and since then, I feel like I've barely slept a wink.

'Another glass?' I offer Fay as I finish the last of my champagne and lean over to fetch the bottle that sits in the cooler.

'I thought we said we weren't going to drink too much,' Fay reminds me. 'We need to keep a clear head and we've got an early start tomorrow.'

'It's just one bottle of champagne. And it's not as if I brought it here. It was a gift, and it'll be rude if we don't drink it, right?'

Fay can't argue too much with that, and as I pick up the bottle, she holds out her glass and accepts a refill.

'Are you okay?' I ask her after refilling our glasses and putting the bottle back down, noting my wife staring absentmindedly out of the window.

'Yeah, fine.'

'You seem a bit distracted.'

'I'm okay.'

I'm not sure I'm buying that, but I won't push the matter, sinking back into the sofa and enjoying the champagne instead.

The silence we sit in there could be a little unnerving to some, but I'm loving it. It makes a difference from my phone ringing incessantly, my email inbox growing fuller by the minute and numerous people trying to see me. I used to wonder who wouldn't want to be a boss, but now I have to ask myself, who would?

Things started going wrong for my company when one client was late in paying their invoice to us, and while one faulty cog shouldn't be capable of breaking a whole machine, in our case, it turned out to be so. They were our biggest client, which meant the money they owed was sizeable, and while we were entitled to raise a claim against them for late payment, the lack of funds triggered several issues in the business. Money drying up in one area meant more had to be found in another, but while I did a good job for a while in keeping all the plates spinning, it got to the point where we were struggling to pay our bills, employees and suppliers. Then we got audited, which is always a nightmare time because rather than focusing on running my business, I was sitting in meeting rooms having to talk through how the whole operation runs with annoying jobsworth types.

Stress. Time constraints. Frustration. On and on it went until it all started to become too much, not just for me, but for Fay too. We've worked ourselves too hard to keep things going, but while this isn't over yet, we needed a break.

I certainly needed this champagne.

I put my head back on the sofa and close my eyes, letting out a deep sigh and telling myself the same thing that I've been telling myself for a while now.

*Everything will be okay. Things will work out in the end. They always do.*

I feel like I could fall asleep right here and probably would have been about to if it wasn't for Fay giving me a nudge and telling me that somebody was on their way to the barn.

'Who is it?' I ask as I sit up and accidentally spill a little of my champagne on the carpet.

'I think it's Logan's wife. She's carrying a cake.'

I get my first glimpse of the woman Fay booked our stay at this barn with then as I spot a brunette woman carrying a covered dish coming along the lawn towards us. My first thought is that she is attractive, though it's a thought I'll keep to myself because I'm not sure Fay would appreciate it. But as my wife often has the habit of doing, she seems to read my mind.

'She's pretty, don't you think?' she asks me accusingly.

'Is she?'

'You don't think she is?'

'Erm, I don't know. Maybe.'

It's hardly the most convincing of answers, but it's something, I suppose.

'I guess we better say hi then,' I figure, putting my glass down and getting up, and Fay follows me to the door, which we open just as the woman arrives.

'Hello. I'm Bridgette, Welcome to the barn house. Are you all settled in?' she says to us with a big smile on her face.

'Yeah, I think so, thank you,' I reply, matching her smile.

'Here's a little welcome present. I hope you enjoy it. It's a Victoria Sponge,' Bridgette says as she hands me the dish.

'Thank you, but you didn't have to do that,' Fay says. 'The champagne was more than enough.'

'It's no trouble. None at all,' Bridgette replies, flashing a dazzling set of white teeth. 'How was your journey down here?'

'Great. Quite easy, actually,' I reply, already looking forward to tucking into the cake just as soon as the woman who baked it for us has gone. But she isn't going anywhere yet and seems quite keen to hang around and chat.

'I hope my husband showed you where everything is. Do you have any questions about anything?' she asks us, still smiling to the point where surely her cheeks must be aching a little bit by now.

'No, we're fine, thank you,' Fay replies. 'We've got everything we need.'

'Yeah, we're good, thanks,' I say, expecting that to be the end of this conversation, and now the host will most likely leave us alone for the rest of our stay. But that doesn't happen. Instead, she surprises Fay and me by asking us a question and, at the same time, extending an invitation our way.

'I don't normally do this, but you seem like a lovely couple, so I thought I'd offer,' Bridgette begins. 'You can say no if you want to, but I was wondering if you might both be interested in joining us for a drink at the house this evening? Nothing too big or fancy. Just sharing company. What do you say?'

I glance at Fay to see what her reaction is, though I already have a feeling what it will be.

She's going to say no and as she goes to open her mouth, I get the impression I'm right. That's why I interject before she can say anything and give an answer myself.

'That would be lovely. Thank you very much,' I say. 'What time would you like us to call by?'

# 6

## FAY

'Why did you do that?' I ask my husband seconds after I have closed the door of the barn and watched Bridgette walking away from us, meaning she is now out of earshot.

'I was just being polite,' he replies with an irritating shrug. 'What's wrong with that?'

'What's wrong with it? We're supposed to be having a quiet night, just the two of us. That's why we came here. What part of that don't you understand?'

'Oh, relax. It's just a drink. It's not the end of the world,' Aidan says as he wanders back over to the champagne bottle and looks to be about to pour himself another drink. That's when I wonder if the alcohol has gone to his head slightly, and that's why he gave Bridgette an answer that was not particularly well thought out. We haven't eaten much today, so drinking on an empty stomach would mean the champagne has had more of an effect on him than it would usually do, and that could have caused him to make a silly decision. Or maybe I'm just being too generous to him, and he was capable of making the silly decision without adding alcohol to the equation.

'Are you serious? You think it's a good idea?' I ask, incredulous because I'm not sure how I've ended up being the only one out of the pair of us who thinks it's a terrible one.

'Yeah, I think so. It'll be nice to have a little company. Take our minds off things.'

'We came here to take our minds off things.'

'I know, and we are still going to spend most of our time in here. But an hour or so up at the house won't hurt, will it? She said to go around at six, so that still gives us over five hours to relax here, just the two of us.'

Aidan slumps back down onto the sofa and takes another sip, seemingly pleased with himself and what he has signed us up for tonight. But I'm still mad at him about this.

'I'm the one who found this place. It was my idea. Now you're ruining it,' I moan, hating the fact that I'm having to complain to him, but I feel like I have a right to. How would he like it if he had gone to the trouble I went to in sorting out our booking here only for me to jump at the first chance to get out of here and be with other people? It's so disrespectful, though he still doesn't see it that way.

'I'm sorry, I was just being polite. It would have been awkward if I said no.'

'Would it? I'm sure she would have got over it.'

'I've said yes now, so what do you want me to do? Go up to their house and say we've changed our mind?'

'No, because then she'll know I've made you say it!' I cry.

'Okay, so I guess we're going then,' Aidan says, looking nonplussed about all this.

'We'll have to now, won't we!'

I turn for the stairs, in a mood and wanting to get some space from my partner, and while Aidan tells me to come and sit with him, I ignore him and go up to the bedroom. When I get there, I lie on the bed and take a deep breath, trying to relax even though I'm still furious at my husband. But it's not easy to calm down for a variety of reasons. That's because I've been harbouring feelings of both annoyance and resentment towards Aidan before we even got here, and that means this is threatening to be the final straw.

I've not said this to him yet because I know it won't do either of us any good if I vocalise it, but I blame him for everything that has happened recently with our business issues and the stress that trying to fix it all has caused us. After all, he was the one who wanted to start the business in the first place, so it's an easy stance for me to take. I was happy enough just being an employee elsewhere. Sure, I'd never have gotten rich that way, but there is more to life than that, and I was happy enough before the money. But Aidan always had his dreams, visions and goals, and after I got talked into going along with them, I can't help but feel it was a mistake.

Our relationship is faltering, there's no doubt about that, but we were great before the business. We never argued, and we certainly never had so much to worry about. But being our own bosses has changed things, and now we've ended up here, what does Aidan do?

*He simply finds another way to make things difficult.*

As I stay lying on the bed, I try to see things from his point of view. It was a nice invitation, and it is just a drink. I can see why he said yes, especially when Bridgette was fluttering her eyelashes at him and smiling so much. He's always been a sucker for a pretty woman, though I did notice how attractive Logan was too, so I suppose I can't be mad at him there. And like Aidan says, we're not expected at the house until six, so we do have many hours before that where it can just be the two of us in this barn.

*Relax. Everything will be fine. Just go downstairs and have another glass of champagne.*

I force myself up off the bed and am about to go downstairs when I look at my small suitcase. I consider unpacking it, but it seems unnecessary as we're only here for one night. But now we have this 'drinks date' to go to, I should probably wear something a little nicer than what I currently have on, so I unzip my case and pull out a few things. I've packed very lightly, but I have a nice blouse I could put on, and I'll apply a little make-up later too, so I take out the small bag with all my accessories in it and place that beside the blouse on the bed.

I'll get ready later, but for now, there's nothing more I need in my case, so I should just zip it back up and go downstairs. But now it's open, I can't resist taking a quick peek at the thing I have buried at the bottom of my suitcase. It's a thing I was not supposed to bring with me and a thing Aidan would go mad at me for if he knew it was here. Bridgette and Logan would also be disappointed because having it with me goes against

their policy of this being a technology-free haven for a true escape from society.
It's my mobile phone and while it's currently turned off, I am massively tempted to turn it on for a quick minute.
*But should I do it?*

I know there's no signal here because that was made clear to me when I booked this place, but I brought the phone with me anyway, just in case I felt I needed to use it and was able to get a signal somewhere. Who knows? Maybe if I walk far enough away from the barn, I could get one, even just for a minute or so. But that's not the point of being here, so I know I should put my phone away and forget all about it.

So why can't I?

Some people who are obsessed with their phones say being without it is like losing a limb, and while I never thought I was that bad, I know now that I'm trying it that it does not feel at all natural to be so disconnected. It's a good thing to try and get away from work for a while, but get away from everything? Family? Friends? Are they things a person should disconnect from? I'm not so sure, but it's a little late for that now because I'm here, and I can't contact them even if I wanted to.

Sitting down on the bed, I turn my phone on just for a second and get confirmation of there being no signal here when I look at the top right-hand corner of the screen. But that doesn't mean this device is totally useless because while I can't send or receive any new messages, I can see the ones that were on here before I went off the grid. There are many messages on my phone, but it's the conversation I was having with my best friend, Natalie, that I find myself re-reading one more time as I sit here and hear Aidan pulling that damn champagne bottle out of the ice bucket again.

Considering that Natalie and I have been best friends for over twenty years, there are plenty of messages on here, a whole history between us, and it's always been one I've cherished because she's always been there for me through the ups and downs of life. But unfortunately, there have been more downs than ups for me lately, and that is why the last few messages I received from my friend were not of the positive kind.

I feel a terrible knot twisting in the pit of my stomach as I sit and re-read Natalie's last few text messages - messages that were hard to read when I first received them and are just as difficult to go over now. That's because she was giving me some home truths and they are never easy things to have to process. But while she said some shocking things, she only said them because she cares about me, and I had to keep that in mind. It's that fact that I am keeping in mind here as I think about Natalie and the advice she gave me recently in my inbox.

***Aidan is trouble.***

***I think you're making a mistake by staying with him.***

***You need to leave him.***

Those were just a few of the things Natalie said to me, not that I agreed with any of them at the time. I know she was just trying to give me advice, but I ignored it all, and I am continuing to ignore it, the proof of that being me here in this barn house with Aidan when Natalie thinks I should be well away from him by now.

So why the harsh opinion of my best friend?

It would be easy to presume that she has never got along with Aidan and harbours an agenda against him like some friends can be like with their mate's partner. But that's not the case here because Natalie had previously got on well with my husband. She found him funny and charming when she met him and even quietly whispered to me once that she wished she'd met him before I had because he was "a real keeper." She was only joking about wanting him for herself, of course, but the bigger point she was making was that she approved of my choice of man, and that meant so much to me, and indeed Aidan, because it's always important for a new partner to get along with the friendship group.

So why the sudden change?

Why has Natalie gone from loving Aidan to loathing him?

*Why does she want me to leave him?*

It's because she realised he wasn't as perfect as he seemed, and it's a realisation that she came to after I had discovered that fact for myself too. What started a few weeks ago with the failing business revealed many of Aidan's flaws - flaws that he had kept so well hidden that nobody knew they existed, least of all me. But once they were exposed, that's when it became apparent to Natalie that he was no longer the right man for me.

As I stare at my phone screen and shake my head, I'm doing so because I know my friend is right, and I've been stupid to ignore her advice. Aidan is trouble, and I should have left him. But now I'm at this barn with him, and he is glugging champagne like everything is alright.

But it's not. I know it, and he should know it too.

*This relationship is doomed.*

It's just a shame my best friend realised it before I did because now I fear it is too late for me to leave him. In fact, doing something as drastic as that could just make things worse for the both of us, and now we've got to go and spend time with our hosts here and pretend like everything is fine between us. Drink their wine. Be entertained by their stories.

All the while, Aidan and I know that we are simply putting on a façade.

# 7

## LOGAN

I have to give my wife some credit. I was sceptical about the idea of renovating the barn and hiring it out to holidaymakers, but it really has been a good money maker. The barn has been booked again, and the couple currently in there are paying us a tidy sum of money to stay for the night, and considering how little effort it takes on our part to get the barn ready these days, it's easy cash.

However, one thing I really wasn't sure about was the idea of making it technology-free and something of a 'retreat' from the stresses of everyday life. I understood the concept my wife was suggesting, but I wasn't sure it was necessary and thought it may even hinder us finding potential customers or 'guests' as Bridgette keeps reminding me to call them.

I thought the barn itself was glamorous enough for people to want to stay there anyway, but people might be put off if they found out there was no Wi-Fi, TV or phone signal. But Bridgette was adamant that was how she wanted to market this place, so, in the end, I went along with it, though I was very much prepared to say 'I told you so' if it turned out to be a disaster and we received no booking requests. But that has not happened, and business at the barn has been steady, not that I get involved in that side of things. I leave all the bookings to Bridgette because this was her baby, her brainchild and her business, so I wouldn't want to interfere. All I do is show the guests to the barn when they get here and occasionally, I'm the one who collects the cash, mainly because Bridgette prefers I do that job while she simply supplies the cake. But that's fine by me. Besides, I have my own job, so that keeps me busy enough.

I invest in stocks and shares and spend several hours a day sitting in my office at the back of this cottage, keeping tabs on the financial markets and making sure I'm making more money than I'm losing. It started as a passion, but I grew it into a full-time job, meaning I could quit the 9-5 and stop commuting and stay at home, which was always the dream, and I do not miss going into London every day. My new job was the main reason we decided to move out here to this cottage in the middle of nowhere. There was no need to be in a busy, built-up area anymore, so Bridgette and I jumped at the chance to get out into the countryside. The old, unused barn at the bottom of the garden was just something that came with the cottage, but my creative wife has revamped that and now we both have a job to keep ourselves occupied out here.

The pair of us don't leave the cottage much, only venturing to the nearest supermarket every now and again to buy our groceries, and barring me stopping off for a quick pint at a pub on the way home, I am quite happy being here. I know Bridgette enjoys our fairly quiet life, too, because she has told me so on several occasions, which makes me happy because you know what they say.

*'Happy wife – Happy life.'*

I met Bridgette when I was still in my old life, the one that consisted of an office job and a dreary commute into a heavily overpopulated area. We got chatting one day while I was sitting in a park near my office. I was having a sandwich and enjoying a rare moment away from my colleagues and clients and after spotting a space beside her on a bench and asking if it was vacant, she invited me to sit down.

I hadn't been planning on striking up a conversation with the woman initially, though I wouldn't have minded the idea of it because I had noticed she was very attractive, and I was single at the time, so why not try my luck? She certainly looked smart sitting there next to me in a buttoned-up blouse and pretty skirt that was long enough to be respectable at her workplace but short enough to make me more intrigued. But it was actually Bridgette who started talking first, asking me if I worked nearby. I confirmed that I did, and after she had asked me what I did for a job, I told her. But trying to impress her, I also made sure to mention my 'side hustle,' which was my tendency to dabble with stocks and shares, and somewhat bragging, I told her that I was actually making enough money there to quit my job, which was something I was seriously considering doing.

As I'd hoped, that greatly impressed the woman, who introduced herself as Bridgette, and we shook hands. I then asked about her, and she told me about her work life, which consisted of being a PA to a very busy and stressed-out man who said he appreciated her but had a funny way of showing it. Like me, I got the impression Bridgette was eager for a change but not just professionally. With no wedding ring on her finger, I wondered if she would be interested in a change in her love life too, and that was why I asked her out on a date that weekend. She said yes; the date went well, and after one thing led to another, we ended up quitting our jobs, getting married and moving out here to the countryside.

All that from me asking to sit on one half of a bench so I could eat my sandwich on my lunch break.

*It's funny how life can be so unpredictable, isn't it?*

But the unpredictability of it all has not ended since then, and I get yet another example of that just now as Bridgette walks into my office and gives me a surprising bit of information.

'I've invited Fay and Aidan for a drink tonight,' she tells me, instantly distracting me from the Excel spreadsheet I was just looking at.

'What? Why?'

'Just being friendly.'

'They're supposed to be on holiday.'

'And they still are. One drink won't ruin that.'

'But we don't even know them.'

'Then let's get to know them.'

Bridgette doesn't seem to have any qualms about a couple of strangers coming into our house later. But I certainly do.

'I wish you'd consulted with me before inviting them,' I say to her in a huff. 'It's my evening as well as yours, and I was looking forward to a quiet one.'

'It will still be a quiet one. It's just a drink.'

'But why? We've never invited anybody here before. They are our customers, not our friends, and we should keep that line very clear.'

'They are guests, not customers,' Bridgette reminds me for the umpteenth time since we started the barn business. 'And I know we have never done this before, but maybe we should because I think it's a very good idea. What better way to guarantee our guests not only leave here happy but also recommend us then to be ultra-hospitable and go the extra mile for those who choose to stay with us.'

I see what my wife is getting at, and she thinks doing this might improve future business, but I'm still not so sure.

'I just don't think it's necessary,' I tell her, shaking my head. 'They've already paid to be here, and they are checked in at the barn. Why can't we just leave them to it? We don't need to go the extra mile, as you say. This was supposed to be more of a passive income thing, not a chore. Now you're telling me we have to entertain these guests tonight.'

'I'll do the entertaining; you just sit and have a drink with us with a smile on your face. You can manage that, right?'

I'm sure I can manage that, but that's not the point.

'I just don't understand. Why this couple? Why ask them and not anyone else? What's so special about them?'

'They just seem nice, I suppose,' Bridgette replies, but there has to be more to it than that because my wife never does anything without it being well thought through. I got plenty of evidence of that when we were wedding planning, property hunting and even when she does something as simple as baking a cake. *There is always a plan, so what is it here?*

'What are you hiding from me?' I ask, and for a moment, Bridgette looks nervous before laughing it off.

'Nothing. I'm just being friendly.'

'As you keep saying.'

'Well, I've told you now, and it's happening, so make sure you're ready for six o'clock when they call around.'

Bridgette goes to leave my office then but just before she does, I have one point to raise with her.

'I thought the whole idea of people staying at the barn was so they had a complete break, not just from technology, but from other people. Don't you worry this will ruin that idea for Fay and Aidan a little bit if they have to come here and make small talk with us?'

'No, and they don't have to come here. They said yes.'

'Because they really wanted to or just because they were being polite?'

'Because they wanted to,' Bridgette replies quickly, but she looks about as convinced of that answer as I am. But what else can I say? My wife has gone ahead and planned this without me and has clearly made her mind up on this and once that's happened, there's no hope for me changing it.

'Fine. Whatever,' I say with a shrug. 'But just for the record, I don't think this is a great idea, and I don't want us doing this with every guest who stays at the barn, okay?'

'Your concerns are duly noted,' Bridgette replies breezily. 'And we won't do it with every guest. Just the cute ones.'

Bridgette gives me a wink then before walking out and while I know she did that to tell me she was joking, I can't help but feel a little uncomfortable. She thinks they are cute? Which one exactly? Fay or Aidan or both of them?

I let out a deep sigh and turn back to my computer screen to face my spreadsheet again, but try as I might, I can't concentrate on the work I was doing before my wife came in here and interrupted me. Working from home can be great, but it can also be very distracting, and now my concentration has been broken, I can't regain it easily.

Standing up and walking over to my office window, I put my hands in my pockets and gaze out over my back garden, my mind instantly soothed by the sight of all the lush green grass and healthy foliage that grows around it on all sides. I can't see the barn from here, which is good because it means those who are staying inside it can't see us either, but I think about the couple down there for a moment and wonder what they are doing now. It's a question I often ponder when other people stay at the barn because let's be honest, there is not a whole lot to do there without access to anything technological.

I imagine I'd be quite bored with nothing to do all day but sit around and talk, read a book or stare out of the window, but the guests who come here seem to find enough to busy themselves, and I guess it does prove that plenty of people long for an existence beyond the realms of social media. Some people don't believe a holiday happened if it didn't end up splashed all over Instagram or Facebook, but people like Fay and Aidan are proving them wrong.

I wonder if they will prove me wrong later by making me see that their coming to our house for a drink tonight was not a bad idea.

I guess I'll find out soon enough.

Either that or I'll finally get to say 'I told you so' to my wife.

# 8

## AIDAN

In hindsight, I probably should have taken it a little easier on the champagne. Then again, I wasn't expecting there to be a bottle waiting for me at check-in, and it would have been rude not to partake, so what was I supposed to do? But it's the middle of the afternoon, and I have a fuzzy head, which is why I've just told Fay that I'm going to go for a walk.

There is a path leading into the woods at the back of this humongous garden and that's what I intend to explore, hoping that a little fresh air will clear my head and have me feeling fresh again for later. But I know it might not be the best look if I just leave the barn without inviting my wife to come with me, so I make sure to do just that, going upstairs to find Fay, who has been loitering up in the bedroom for a while now. When I find her, she is lying on the bed and when I realise that she is asleep, I make sure to tread much more quietly.

I hadn't realised she had fallen asleep, but that explains why she's been up here for so long. There I was downstairs thinking she was mad at me for accepting Bridgette's drink invitation, but it seems my wife was just feeling sleepy, so that's a relief.

Watching my very own sleeping beauty for a moment, I smile at how peaceful and still she looks before spotting a blanket on a small chair in front of a dressing table over by the window. Picking up the blanket, I unfurl it before carefully placing it down on top of Fay, ensuring that she isn't going to be cold when she wakes up, whenever that may be.

With my wife clearly preoccupied, I am free to leave the barn by myself so I do just that, putting my boots and coat on and stepping outside before quietly closing the door behind me and then setting off towards the woods. I'm intrigued to see where the path at the bottom of this garden goes, but I am not expecting to see any people on the route because we're so far from anywhere else. It's almost as if Bridgette and Logan have their own private woodland that came with their property based on how this part of the trail is only accessed from their land, and that only adds to the allure of this place, as well as adding to the price tag of it, I imagine.

Starting the trail and entering the woods, things get a little darker as the pale sunlight is partially blocked out by the tree canopy overhead. But I can still see where I am going easily enough, and the further I walk, the more I am glad I got out of the barn for some exercise. Being able to stretch my legs is just what I need after being sat in a car for such a long time to get here, and the exercise is certainly helping me clear out the champagne-induced brain fog that had come over me. But getting out of the barn for a short break was something I'd been hoping to get the chance to do at some point during my stay here, and ideally, I would get to do it alone, which is fortunately what I've managed to do. I'd have happily gone for a walk with Fay if she had been awake, but if I'm honest, I was quite glad to see that she was asleep because it's given me a chance to have a little privacy, something that has been sorely lacking since we left our home county yesterday.

And why do I need privacy?

*So I can do something I'm not supposed to do.*

Looking up the trail ahead of me to make sure nobody is coming before glancing back over my shoulder to check that no one is behind me either, I reach into my pocket and take out my new mobile phone, the one that my wife does not know about.

I purchased this particular device at the service station we stopped at this morning. While Fay was waiting for me in the car after I told her I was just getting a few more snacks, I went into the phone shop there and bought this very basic handset with a cheap pay-as-you-go sim card and now I have it, it means I can make a call or text without my wife seeing it.

*All I need to do now is find a phone signal.*

I have no idea if I will get one around here, but I'm planning on walking far enough along this trail to try my luck. If not, then it's not the end of the world, but if I can find a signal, then it would be helpful. It would be helpful because there is a person I could do with contacting because I know they'll be missing me right about now.

That person is Lana, the accounts assistant I hired for my business last year and a person I have grown very close to since then. That's because Lana and I didn't exactly keep our relationship professional when we started working alongside each other, and that's probably putting it a little mildly. The truth is that we were engaged in an affair, one that started late one night when it was just the two of us at the office and one that only ended recently, unfortunately, on very acrimonious terms.

I know I should consider myself lucky that Fay is here with me now after what I did with Lana because my wife did discover the affair in the end. But I'm not a totally bad guy. I do love my wife and want things to work out between us and my being here with her should prove that. If anything, I'd say I'm almost too caring because rather than just ignore Lana and cut her off, I am hoping to try and make contact with her today to see if she is okay. I know she's been stressed about how things ended between me and her and also how things ended with her and my business too, her role in my accounts team being terminated upon Fay's request when the affair was exposed.

Despite being over fifteen years my junior, Lana is very mature - possibly more mature than me, though that's not saying much. She didn't deserve to be messed around by me, but then again, Fay didn't deserve what I and one of our employees have been doing behind her back either. But like many things in life, things don't always go to plan, and the affair just happened, just like the downturn in my business just happened and also like just how me accepting Bridgette's invite for a drink tonight just happened too.

Checking my new and very cheap phone, I don't see a signal yet, so I keep walking, and I'm well into the woods now, far away from the barn and the main house and the people who reside in them. As suspected, I haven't seen a single person out here in these woods since I entered them, but it is a little creepy being so alone. Things only get creepier when I hear a twig snapping nearby.

*Is somebody else out here with me?*

I look around but can't see anybody, so I carry on, returning my focus to my phone. It's a model very reminiscent of the first ever mobile I got back when portable phones first came on the market. That shows how basic and antiquated this handset is, but I don't need it to do much. I just need it to allow me to make a phone call to the number I know by heart now.

Lana's number.

*And then I get it.*

It's just one bar, but it's proof that there might be signal around here if I keep looking for it, so I forge on, and sure enough, I soon get two bars of signal strength in the top corner of the screen. That might be just enough for me to make a call, so I type in Lana's number and then press the device to my ear, hoping she answers me because I can't spend all day hanging out here in the middle of these woods.

I can hear cars zooming along a road somewhere in the distance, so I guess that is on the other side of the woods, but I stay where I am as I wait for Lana to answer.

*But will she?*

'Hello?'

The voice is distant but clear enough for me to hear, though when I do, I'm not sure it sounds like Lana.

'Hey, Lana? It's me.'

'Who is this?'

The male voice at the other end of the line is disconcerting and I don't know what to say. Who is this man and why has he answered Lana's phone? Is he a boyfriend? If so, this could be very awkward.

There's a brief pause at the other end of the line before the stranger asks another question.

'Why are you calling this number?'

I'm not sure I want to answer that until I know who I am speaking to.

'Where's Lana?' I ask again, making it clear I know this is not her. But I could not have prepared myself for what I would hear next.

'This is Detective Stevenson, and I'm with the Yorkshire Police.'

'The police?'

'Yes, now I'm going to-'

I don't hear any more of what the detective has to say because I panic then and hang up.

I know it's not the most mature thing to do, but I've done it now, and the reason I did is because there was something in the detective's voice that told me I could easily talk myself into trouble if I gave my name. To make sure I can't be called back, I turn off the phone quickly before stuffing it back into my pocket.

Calling Lana, or at least trying to reach her, was a mistake, and I regret it instantly. I was only trying to have another go at making her see that I didn't mean for any of what had happened to occur and that I wish things had been different. I've tried telling her that several times before and while it hasn't worked, I thought one more go might help. But not only did I not get to speak to her, I got something worse.

Why was a detective answering Lana's phone?

Why didn't she answer it herself?

What is going on back home?

Is she ok?

I don't have any of those answers as I make my way back to the barn, but I do know one thing for sure.

I'm not going to mention this to Fay when she wakes up.

# 9

## FAY

Pretending to be asleep when I heard Aidan coming upstairs in the barn is not something I'm particularly proud of, but I did it anyway to avoid talking to him at that time. He obviously fell for my little performance because he put a blanket over me, which was a nice gesture, I suppose, before I heard him leaving the barn shortly afterwards.

I guess he's gone for a walk into the woods along that trail, but I doubt there is much of interest to see out there, so I'm sure he'll be back soon, and when he returns, I don't think it would be good if I just carried on pretending to sleep. That's why I have forced myself up off the bed, and after folding the blanket and returning it to where it belongs on the chair by the dressing table, I go downstairs and step outside to have a look for my husband.

But while I do see somebody in the big back garden, it's not the man I'm looking for.

It's Logan. The male owner of this lovely property that we are staying in is over on the other side of the garden, using hedge clippers to trim one of the many bushes that surround this place. He doesn't notice me watching him at first, so I get several seconds of admiring his work with his swift, sharp technique, not to mention his muscular forearms operating the garden instrument with ease. But he turns around suddenly, possibly getting that 'sixth sense' that somebody has eyes on him, and when he sees me standing outside the barn, he lowers the hedge clippers and gives me a friendly wave.

I make sure to wave back before swiftly returning to the cosy interior of the barn, not wanting to linger too long out here and either make Logan feel uncomfortable at being watched or make him feel like he has to wander over to me and start a conversation. We'll have plenty of time for that later when we go up to the house for a drink, so best not to potentially burn through too many topics of conversation with him before then.

As I close the barn door behind me, I wonder what Logan thought about his wife inviting us to theirs later. Did she discuss the idea with him beforehand, or was it as much of a surprise to him as it was to me? Then again, maybe it's an invitation that they extend to all their guests. I wonder what the ratio is between those who say yes and those who say no.

Would Aidan and I have been the first to refuse a drink with them?

*Or are we the first to say yes?*

I try not to concern myself with that question too much as I clear up the empty champagne bottle and put the two glasses in the dishwasher. No wonder Aidan needed some fresh air. He drank most of this bottle himself.

Shaking my head because I can't believe I was naïve enough to think he would stick to his promise of not drinking alcohol during our trip, I unpack a few of the grocery items we picked up at the service station earlier. It's nothing much, just some basics to make a sandwich and some milk to make tea, and it's a cup of tea that I make next after I locate the box of teabags in the cupboard above the kettle.

As I wait for the kettle to boil, I hear Aidan returning.

'Hey, you're awake! How was your nap?' he asks me when he finds me in the kitchen pouring hot water into a cup.

'Yeah, it was nice,' I say, telling a white lie before I offer him a tea too.

'That would be great, thanks,' he replies, and after I have handed him his drink, we go into the lounge area and take a seat.

'So, where did you go?' I ask him.

'Just down that trail into the woods.'

'You didn't go too far?'

'No.'

'See anything interesting?'

'Not really. Just a lot of trees.'

'Sounds like a wood to me.'

I give Aidan a wry smile and as he smiles back at me, I remind myself once again that things are going to be okay, even if, most of the time, it doesn't seem like they will be.

'So, what are you going to wear for our event this evening?' Aidan asks me as he puts his arm around me, and we snuggle on the sofa.

'I have absolutely no idea. Dressing to impress was not high on my list of priorities when I packed to come here.'

'You didn't want to make an effort for your husband? Charming.'

'You know what I mean. We were supposed to be staying in, just the two of us.'

'I know, I'm only teasing. We don't have to stay for long.'

'I wonder what their motive is for inviting us to the house,' I ponder then.

'Motive? What do you mean?'

'I mean, are they really just being nice, or is there something they want?'

'What could they want?'

'I don't know. Us?'

'What do you mean?'

'What if they're swingers, and this is just part of their routine? They get a couple to stay in their barn house, invite them up for a friendly drink and then suggest a little partner swapping.'

Aidan almost chokes on his tea when he hears my suggestion.

'You're kidding. You think that's why they invited us?'

'No, of course not. I was joking! Why? Do you?'

'No!'

The pair of us are in hysterics now, greatly amused by the idea of Bridgette and Logan having sinful intentions with us. But neither of us actually thinks that could be the case, which is a relief, otherwise we most definitely would not be going to meet them for a drink.

The rest of the afternoon passes peacefully enough with neither me nor Aidan straying far from the sofa, content to sit beside one another and talk about all manner of things, from events in our distant past when things were much simpler to those we hope might happen in our future when things could be perfect again. It's a pleasant way to spend a couple of hours, and while I know there is still an undercurrent that exists between us, one that makes me wonder if we are going to be okay or not in the long run, I manage to mostly do what I came here to do.

*Unwind.*

So much so that before we know it, we've lost track of time, and when Aidan tells me it is half past five, I figure we better get up and get ourselves ready for our drinks date.

I plan to get changed and apply a little make-up while Aidan goes for a shower and as I do that, I think I overreacted a little earlier. Maybe going for a drink will be fun for the two of us, and it sure has been a while since we had any of that. What's more, it might be quite fascinating to learn a little about Bridgette and Logan and what their lives are like beyond them just being a couple who rent out their barn house to needy souls. I might learn something interesting tonight but if not, it will at least take my mind off things even more.

The only thing I'm missing now is a little music because that's always a good thing to listen to while getting ready to go out, but alas, this being a technology-free place has put paid to that. I could always turn my phone on again and play some of the songs that I have saved on there, but that would alert Aidan to the fact that I have my phone with me, so I'll leave it in the suitcase to be safe.

I guess I'll just have to make my own music then, so that's what I do, starting to hum to myself before breaking out into a full song a few minutes later, and by the time Aidan has got out of the shower and come into the bedroom to get dressed, I am really going for it, singing loud and proud.

'Wow, someone's in a good mood,' Aidan observes as he dries his wet hair with a towel, and I flash him a wink through the reflection in the mirror of the dressing table I am sitting at.

It's a wink that reminds him that I can be fun and carefree like him at times, even if it has always been harder for me to be that way too often. But I'm making an effort to be that way tonight because I want this to be an enjoyable evening.

Little did I know it then but 'enjoyable' was not quite the word to describe what it would be.

*'Eventful' would have been far more apt.*

# 10

## BRIDGETTE

While I had no issues giving my prisoner in the basement a very dry cheese sandwich to eat earlier, that just won't do for Fay and Aidan, so I'm making far more of an effort in what I am preparing for them.

'A cheeseboard? Don't you think that's a bit much?' Logan says when he walks into the kitchen and sees me carefully laying out a veritable selection of cheeses on a stylish wooden tray alongside a bunch of grapes and some biscuits.

'It's no trouble,' I reply, which is a bit of a lie, but it's not that big of a deal. 'We're having red wine, so why not have something to accompany it?'

'Have you even asked if they drink wine?' is my husband's next question, but I don't have time for him picking holes in my plan, so I brush off his concerns and tell him to go and make sure the lounge area is looking tidy.

'Anyone would think the King is coming for dinner,' Logan moans as he leaves the kitchen to go and do as I tell him, but that's just something he always says whenever I ask him to make sure the place is looking presentable ahead of any guests arriving.

With him out of the way again, I am able to finish working on my presentation of the cheeseboard before I leave the kitchen myself and go upstairs to my bedroom, where I plan to quickly get ready so that I'm looking just as presentable as the house.

Taking off my baggy jeans and jumper, I slip into something that says I have made a bit more of an effort with my appearance, putting on a blouse and a pair of tighter jeans, an outfit that does a better job of accentuating my curves, a treat for both Logan and indeed, Aidan, if he should happen to care to look. Once that's done, then I quickly comb my hair before applying a little make-up and putting in my earrings, and it's amazing how quickly I can transform myself from a dowdy housewife to a fairly appealing woman who looks to be flourishing in her forties.

I used to be envious of men and how little upkeep their appearances required when we were younger, but now that I'm older, I realise that women possess far more in their bag of tricks to de-age themselves, which is often why we can still look good as we advance in years while men have far less to cover up their grey hairs and wrinkles with.

It does feel good to make an effort with my appearance, and it also feels good to know that there is a woman in my basement right now who would do anything to make herself look and feel better. But there's not much she can do about that, and while I'm up here beautifying myself, she is down there wallowing beside the leftover crusts of her bland cheese sandwich.

Once I'm satisfied that I'm looking good, I leave the bedroom and go back downstairs to check on Logan and when I do, I find him plumping up the cushions on the sofa like the well-trained and obedient man that he is.

'Wow, you look great,' he tells me when he sees me standing in the doorway, and I make sure to return the compliment before I thank him for tidying up.

'They should be here any minute,' I say after glancing at the clock on the mantelpiece, and I hurry back to the kitchen to not only check on the cheeseboard and make sure it has everything on it that it needs to have, but also to get the wine ready.

There is a particular bottle of red that I have had in mind since Aidan first accepted my invitation, and that's the one I pull off the rack now. Slicing the foil around the bottle top with the small blade on the bottle opener, I then proceed to open it, expertly removing the cork with the minimum of fuss because this is something I've done many a time over the last few years since I started dating Logan and he introduced me to the pleasure of a good bottle of wine. Before I met him, I was more of a vodka drinker, and it was cheap vodka at that. But my life has levelled up in more ways than one since I met Logan in a park one sunny lunchtime during the working week. But I can't help but feel a tiny pang of guilt as I think back on that first meeting with my now husband because while many happy times have come from it, it did all begin based on a lie.

*My lie.*

When Logan asked if he could sit down next to me on that bench in the park, I'm sure he presumed I was just like him in that I was yet another office worker taking a break for lunch. But despite being dressed in typical office attire and also despite telling Logan that I worked as a personal assistant in an office not far from the park, that was not the truth at all. The truth was that at that time, I was completely jobless and only prevented from being homeless by a scheme that allowed me to have a place to stay until I was able to find work. It was at that place that I made a few friends and one of those was kind enough to lend me some formal attire to wear, as the idea was that I was supposed to attend job interviews to find myself an occupation. But I didn't do that. Working for an employer had never appealed to me, not as a young woman and certainly not as an older one, so instead of going to interviews, I went to the park, and I went there with one goal in mind.

I was going to meet a man.

But not just any man.

*A man with the financial means to change my life.*

I had no idea that man would be Logan when he asked to sit down on the bench next to me. All I knew was that a pretty woman sitting alone on a bench in a busy park stood as good a chance as anybody of having a man try and strike up a conversation with her. And so it proved. Logan made a little small talk before we got to know each other better, and after I had fed him a lie about where I worked and he had told me what I hoped to be the truth of him making money in stocks and shares as a hobby that would soon be a full-time job, I agreed to go on a date with him.

My husband, bless him, is a good man, but he is a flawed man, and perhaps his biggest flaw is that he underestimates me so much. Not only does he not know about the presence of the woman in our basement, but

I'm sure he thinks he is a bit of a knight in shining armour who plucked me from a poorly paid profession and gave me this dream life in a big house in the country. I'm sure it's something that makes him feel all warm and fuzzy inside whenever he thinks about it and while it's a load of nonsense, I'm more than happy for him to carry on thinking that if it makes him happy.

It's certainly more preferable than him knowing the truth.

*It's far better than him knowing who I really am.*

With the wine uncorked, the next job is to take out four glasses and I do just that, setting each of them down beside the open bottle, but I will wait for our guests to arrive before I pour. I will do that for two reasons. One, I have to make sure that each of them likes red wine; otherwise, I need to be prepared to offer them something else. Two, and this is by far the more important reason why I have to wait before I pour - *I need to make sure that the glass with the sedative in it goes to the right person.*

Opening the cupboard in front of me, I make a quick check on the small vial of sedatives that I have been hiding in there, the one that sits behind the dishwasher tablets, a place where Logan would never think to look for anything. The vial is there, but soon it will come out of this cupboard, and the contents of it will go into one of these glasses of wine.

When it does, that's when the games will really begin.

A minute later and there is a knock at the front door and that tells me that our guests have just arrived. It's six o'clock on the button. How prompt of them. Then again, they haven't had far to come, making the short walk up from the barn to the cottage.

Now they are here.

*It's time to get this party started.*

# 11

## FAY

*Just one drink.* That's what I said to Aidan as we left the barn house and made our way up the garden to see Bridgette and Logan. One drink is just enough to be polite and friendly but also enough to ensure we don't end up staying for too long. It's not that I'm bothered about potentially outstaying our welcome, it's more that I don't want to go at all, and as Aidan knocks on the front door, I remind him once again just so he is crystal clear on this.

'Just one drink.'

Aidan nods his head to confirm he has received the message loud and clear, but he looks a little grumpy about it, just like how grumpy he was when I told him to put on the glasses he should be wearing. They are new, which means he's not used to them, but he has them on his face now, and he knows it's for the best, despite him moaning about how they make him look like a nerd.

As Aidan fidgets again with his new eyewear, the door opens, and we see Logan smiling at us from inside what looks like a very warm and welcoming hallway.

'Hey guys, thanks for calling by. Hope you didn't have too long of a journey.'

It's a lame joke considering Logan knows we have literally just walked here from the bottom of his garden, but Aidan and I make sure to be polite and laugh at it before he ushers us inside, and we step into the house. Once in, I see that it is tastefully decorated, although I could have already guessed it would be based on the elegant interior of the barn house too.

This couple have money, and they sure know how to spend it.

'How was your afternoon?' Logan asks us as we take off our shoes, again to be polite.

'Great. We didn't do too much,' Aidan replies.

'That was the plan when you came here, right?' Logan checks, and I tell him it was.

'Yeah, we just wanted to have a quiet time and we've certainly had that,' I reply.

As Aidan tells Logan about his walk in the woods while I was 'asleep', I look around for any sign of Bridgette. But I can't see her yet, though I'm sure she must be lurking somewhere. After all, it was her idea to invite us here, so I doubt she'll leave her husband to do the entertaining by himself for too long.

Sure enough, a few seconds later, I hear her voice from another room.

'Welcome! Welcome!' Bridgette says as she enters the hallway with her arms out wide and a big smile on her face, and based on her enthusiasm, either she hosts all the time and is well versed at having guests over or she doesn't get this opportunity much and is being a little too keen.

Now she's giving Aidan a hug but when she gives me one, I smell a little alcohol on her breath which might explain her level of exuberance. But she clearly wants to bring us up to that same level.

'Can I get you guys a drink?' she asks. 'How does red wine sound?'

'It sounds perfect,' Aidan replies quickly, and once I've confirmed that I'm game for a little wine too, Bridgette scurries away into what I presume is the kitchen to fetch us our drinks. While she does that, Logan shows us into the lounge area, and what a lounge area it is.

Two sofas and an armchair sit in front of a roaring log fire, and it's as cosy in here as it is warm. While I'm admiring the fire, Logan adds another log to it before inviting us to take a seat. As we do, Bridgette reappears with our drinks and hands Aidan his glass before furnishing me with mine.

'Thanks for coming,' she says with a big smile. 'We don't do this with many of our guests, do we?'

She looks to Logan then and he confirms that it is true.

I do feel like asking what is so special about us but decide not to, and a moment later, Bridgette is gone again, leaving the room to go and get something else.
*But what?*

'Lovely place you have here,' Aidan observes before he takes a glug of his wine. 'We always wanted a fire in our house, didn't we?'

Aidan looks at me, and I nod before taking a sip of my own drink and watching the orange flames flickering before us.

'I feel it really adds character to a room,' Logan muses, and I couldn't agree more with him as Bridgette returns, this time carrying a cheeseboard.

'Just a little something to nibble on while we have our drinks,' she says as she places it down on the coffee table between the two sofas, and while the cheese, grapes and crackers do look appealing, I tell her that she did not need to make a fuss for us. But she says it is no trouble at all.

I'm not sure if that is strictly true, but it's a nice touch, and Aidan is not shy in tucking in as he sits forward and picks up a knife.

'Lovely,' he says as Bridgette gives Logan a drink, and the man of the house settles into the armchair, a chair I suspect he spends a lot of time sitting in because he sure does look comfortable once he's in it.

This is all very nice and hospitable, but I am still feeling a little awkward, as well as unsure as to why we are here, but Bridgette is showing no signs of any awkwardness herself, encouraging Aidan to put more cheese on his cracker while telling him there is plenty more wine when he's ready for it.

We've only been here five minutes, but I'm already struggling to see how Aidan is going to keep to our "one drink" policy, though I'll still be trying my best to stick to the plan. But perhaps sensing my reluctance to stay and enjoy ourselves here too long, Bridgette offers me something else to eat when she sees I haven't touched the cheese.

'Oh, no, I'm fine, thank you,' I say before Bridgette tells Logan to put some music on.

While he does that, Aidan asks the couple a few things about this house. How long they've lived here for. If they enjoy being so remote. Why they decided to share their lovely land with others instead of just keeping it all for themselves.

Bridgette fields all the questions as the music starts to play but while that's happening, I get my first sense of what this might be about.

*I think this couple are lonely.*

It makes sense. There's nobody else around here, and it must get a little boring only having the same person to talk to all the time. I can imagine the conversation gets pretty stale, so this is why they need this injection of fresh chatter into their lives. It might even be why they decided to hire out the barn house. It gives them something else to focus on.

I am feeling quite pleased with myself about having this couple all figured out, though that starts to change a moment later. That's when Bridgette suggests Logan shows Aidan his games room and, more specifically, the full-size pool table he has in there.

While my sports-mad husband excitedly leaves the room with Logan to go and have a game of pool, I am left alone with Bridgette, and for a brief moment, the only sound between us is the crackling of the fire. As I scour my mind for something, anything, to say to break the potentially awkward silence, Bridgette suddenly puts down her glass of wine, leans in closer to me and speaks quietly.

'Would you like to see something?' she asks me, her voice barely audible over the fire.

'Erm, what is it?' I ask, wondering why she's suddenly gone from talking at a normal volume to practically whispering.

'It's something quite unusual.'

'Oh, okay. Erm.'

*What the hell does Bridgette want to show me?*

'Where is it?' I ask, looking around the room in case it might be in here.

'It's in the basement,' Bridgette replies, her voice still very hushed.

'The basement?'

'Yes, that's right. Let's go.'

Bridgette stands then and gestures for me to do the same, but I stay where I am for the time being because this feels very weird.

'What's the matter?' she asks me when she sees my reluctance to move.

'Erm. Nothing. I'm just quite comfortable in front of the fire. It's lovely and warm.'

It's not my best work, but it's the excuse I have come up with to justify staying in my seat. Anything to not have to go and look at something unusual in Bridgette's basement because it just sounds like a weird thing to do.

What could she possibly have to show me down there, and why is it unusual?

A weird work of art? Some sculpture she purchased on a whim? Or something else?

*Something more sinister?*

'We'll come back and sit in front of the fire soon. Just come and have a look at this.'

Bridgette walks out of the room then, and I'm left sitting by myself, wondering what is going on here. For some reason, my instincts aren't just telling me not to follow her. Instead, they are telling me to get out of this house. But why? And I can't just go because it would come across as incredibly rude. Besides, Aidan is not with me. He's in the games room, wherever that is. I can't leave without him.

'Fay?'

Bridgette reappears in the doorway, still wanting me to follow her.

*So I do.*

I put down my glass of wine, stand up and walk towards her. I follow her as she leads me to a door before watching her take out a key and put it into the lock. But just before she turns it, she does something that makes this even more strange.

She puts a finger to her lips.

*Whatever this is, she clearly doesn't want anyone but me to know about it.*

# 12

## AIDAN

The white cue ball clatters loudly into the pack of red and yellow balls, sending them all fanning out across the table in a totally unorganised way. But that is the idea of 'the break' in pool, and as two of the balls drop into the pockets, I get the impression that Logan has spent a lot of time playing this game.

As the owner of this pool table prepares to take his next shot, I look around this games room and feel a wistful longing because, like the man I am currently playing against, I always wanted a room like this in my house too. Unfortunately, only one of us has got their wish, and it isn't me.

'Good shot,' I say as Logan pots another ball, and he thanks me before putting a little chalk onto the tip of his cue and then leaning over the table to strike the cue ball once more.

As he pots yet another ball, I'm beginning to wonder if I'm even going to get a chance to take a shot myself before Logan has potted all his balls along with the black ball to win the game. But then he misses, and I'm up.

Rising off the stool I've just been perched on, I approach the table but as I do, I feel a wave of dizziness wash over me, causing me to pause slightly and put a hand to my head.

'Are you okay?' Logan asks me, clearly having noticed that something might be wrong, but I tell him

I'm fine, and I think I am because the bout of dizziness has passed already.

That was weird, I think, but I don't spend too much time pondering what might have caused it because I have a tricky shot to negotiate here, and I want to start potting a few balls before Logan comes to the conclusion that I'm not a worthy opponent for him at this particular game.

Thankfully, I make the shot, and one of my balls drops into a pocket, and Logan is quick to return the compliment that I just gave him a moment ago.

As I make my way around the table, I glance at one of the numerous items of memorabilia that hang on the wall in this impressive room and see yet another signed photo from a well-known sports star. This room is full of them, and Logan already spent five minutes showing me a few of the things he has in his collection, meaning the pool table in the centre of this room is not the only impressive thing in here.

'I always wanted a games room,' I say as I prepare to take my next shot.

'What's stopped you?' Logan asks as I miss, and he eagerly approaches the table to have another go.

'A few things. Time to set it all up. The space to do it in. The money to make it how I want it. And then, of course, needing to get permission from my wife.'

'Ahh yes, that's always the trickiest part of the equation,' Logan chuckles as he pots another ball. 'You can have all the other things, but until you've got permission from your partner, then it's just a dream.'

'That is true. Like many other things, I guess.'

'What do you mean?' Logan asks me as he makes yet another successful shot, and one more ball disappears from the table.

'Oh, you know. It can be anything. A plan for a house. A business idea. Even a suggestion on where to go on holiday. They're all just dreams until you can get your wife to agree with them.'

Logan seems to know what I am talking about but he also mustn't have too much of a problem getting his wife to be on board with his visions if he managed to make himself a room like this in their house.

'What's your secret?' I ask him as he goes to take another shot.

'My secret?'

'Yeah. How did you get Bridgette to agree to this room?'

'Oh, that was easy. She knew it was important to me, so she had no objections.'

'None at all?'

'Well, a couple of minor ones, but that's just normal, I guess. But she saw how much I wanted a room like this, so ultimately, she wasn't going to stand in my way. Just like I didn't stand in her way when she suggested renovating the barn and renting it out. I guess that's the idea of a successful relationship, isn't it? Both parties need to support the other one in what they want to do.'

Logan is right, but I'm envious that his experience of relationships seems to differ from mine. I've always had a harder task in getting my partners to go along with my dreams. Fay has been the one who has come closest to giving me what I want, which is why I married her and not any of the women from my past, but she has certainly shot down plenty of my ideas over the years too. Some would say for good reason, and maybe a few of my ideas were a little unrealistic, especially where business was concerned, but then again, you have to be somewhat unrealistic before you can do something amazing, right?

As Logan pots another ball and the cue ball rolls perfectly into position for his next shot, I go to take a seat again on the bar stool, but as I turn, I feel dizzy once more.

*Damn it, what is going on?*

I reach out towards the table that my glass of wine sits on to steady myself, and while it takes a little longer than the first time, the dizziness does fade again. But that's twice it's happened now since I came into this room, and I'm worried it might happen again.

I'm not sure what could be causing it. It's not the wine because I've only drunk half the glass that Bridgette gave me. I've been sipping my drink more slowly than I usually would, simply for the fact that Fay insisted on us having only one beverage here, so I'm trying to make it last as long as I can. But the slow speed at which I'm drinking tells me my light-headedness cannot be caused by an overindulgence of alcohol, and as I pick my glass up again and take another sip, I feel calmed somewhat by the smooth liquid.

'This is really good wine,' I say to Logan as he misses what looked to be the easiest shot he's had since our game began.

'Thanks. I'll have to pass on your compliment to Bridgette. She's the one who buys the wine. She's turning into somewhat of a connoisseur, actually. Took an online course in it and everything. I'm more of a beer drinker myself, but I agree, this wine does taste good.'

I'm just about to reply to that when I get another bout of dizziness, but this one is so bad that it causes me to stumble into the table beside me and as I do, my glass of wine actually topples over and the rich, red contents spill onto the floor.

'I'm so sorry,' I say as I realise what I've just done, but despite wanting to pick up the glass that is now threatening to roll off the table and fall to the floor, I cannot seem to get my hands working properly enough to do it in time.

Without me being able to intervene, the glass rolls off the table and shatters loudly on the stone floor of the games room, and as Logan asks me if I am okay, I have already realised that I am most certainly not.

Something is wrong, seriously wrong. Not only do I feel dizzy, but my body is not working as it should be. My movements are slow and stiff, and if I had to compare it to anything, I'd say I feel like I've had multiple shots of tequila and am now at the stage of drunkenness when I need to lie down in a dark room before everything starts spinning and I get sick. But I'm not drunk. I've only had half my wine and the rest of it is splattered all over the floor by my feet.

'Woah, buddy, I think you need to sit down,' Logan says as he suddenly grips my arm, just in time to stop me from stumbling backwards into the wall.

I almost fell over then, but Logan caught me, and as he helps me onto the stool, I hope sitting down will be the thing that helps me regain my equilibrium. But sadly that does not seem to be the thing that does the trick because I'm feeling worse than ever, and I'm at the point where I'm thinking that Logan shouldn't just call Fay to come in here and check on me.

*He should call for an ambulance instead.*

'I donnn'tttt knnnoooow whatzzz happeninnggg tooooo meeee,' I mumble, realising that all my words are slurred, and then it happens.

The dreaded room spin.

I think I'm going to be sick.

*Worse, I think I am going to fall off this stool and onto the hard floor below it.*

Reaching out to Logan in desperation, my hand harmlessly slides down his arm as I lose my balance and fall forward and as I go, I try to brace myself for the impact of hitting the ground.

But the funny thing is that I don't end up feeling anything.

That's because I'm already unconscious before I even make it to the floor.

# 13

## BRIDGETTE

My adrenaline levels are spiking as I lead Fay down the stairs into the basement because I know there is only another second or two to go before she sees what I have to show her down here. There's absolutely no way the woman behind me will be prepared for what is to come but she doesn't need to be. I'm the only one who needed to plan this all out, and everything has gone well so far.

Aidan's drink has been drugged, so he should be well on his way to unconsciousness now, and that just leaves his wife to me, not that I have any plans to drug her.

I need Fay wide awake and fully functioning.

*And she's certainly going to be wide awake when she sees what I keep in this basement.*

As I reach the bottom of the stairs and see Holly first, I quickly step to the side so that when Fay stands next to me, I can move behind her and block her from making a swift exit back up these stairs. I imagine running out of here will be the first thing she wants to do when she sees my prisoner, and I couldn't really blame her for that, but I can't have her getting out of here.

*Not until she has done what I want her to do.*

'Oh my God!' Fay cries when she sees the woman I have trapped down here, and sure enough, her first reaction is to recoil in horror and try and get out of this basement. But I block her exit route before telling her to calm down and saying that I can explain.

Funnily enough, me telling Fay to relax and explaining why I have a terrified woman at my mercy down here does not do the job of calming her down, and she begins to shout out for her husband. But that's a bad idea.

'He can't hear you. This basement is soundproof,' I tell Fay, and not only does she stop shouting when she hears me say that, but she also looks even more afraid than she did a couple of seconds ago.

'What is going on? What are you doing?' Fay asks me as she looks back at Holly who is on her feet and predictably already begging the unexpected visitor for help.

'As I said, I can explain,' I say in between Holly's cries. 'But first, I need you to calm down because you getting all worked up is not going to help anybody, least of all your husband.'

That snaps Fay out of her disbelief.

'Aidan?'

'Yes, he needs your help, so I suggest you listen to what I have to say.'

'What have you done to him?' Fay cries before trying to get past me again, but I surprise her with my strength and shove her backwards away from the stairs. Like many people before her, she was not expecting a woman of my fairly diminutive stature to be able to hold her ground. But I've spent my whole life surprising people, and I'm not going to stop now.

'Aidan will be unconscious in a minute or two, if he isn't already,' I say as Fay's eyes go wide with fear. 'But don't worry, he will wake up soon enough and be okay, at least in the short term. But as for the long term, that depends on you and whether or not you are willing to do what I say.'

'What have you done to him?' Fay cries, furious and fearful. 'And what have you done to her?'

She points at Holly - not that Fay will have any idea what my prisoner's name is or how she ended up down here, though I hope to enlighten her on those matters just as soon as she shuts up and listens to me.

'I just put a little something in Aidan's drink to send him off to sleep,' I tell Fay. 'But as I said, he will be absolutely fine. But the same cannot be said of the woman down here with us. That's where you come in, Fay. I need you to calm down and listen to me carefully because believe me when I say this, your husband's life depends on it.'

Fay finally gets the message now that I am deadly serious, and Aidan needs her to do what I say, so she refrains from making any more panicked statements.

'Good, thank you,' I tell her, maintaining my position in between her and the stairs because she still might try and run. 'Now let me tell you what's going on here and once I have, you will see that I am just like you, Fay. I am someone who loves my husband and wants to protect my relationship, and I am someone who is willing to do anything to achieve that aim. Let me explain.'

I gesture then to Holly, and Fay nervously looks at my prisoner, who is still asking for help in her worn out voice. But that voice is getting on my nerves, so I decide to do something about it and step forward and pull the handkerchief from my pocket before stuffing it into Holly's mouth.

That does the trick and now I can make myself heard more easily, which is important because I have a lot to say to the stunned woman standing nearby.

'This woman you see before you is not a good woman,' I say to Fay as I glare into Holly's tearful eyes. 'This woman does not respect the institution of marriage, and I know that because she had no qualms sleeping with my husband, even though he had a wedding ring on his hand. Just in case you think she could have missed the presence of a ring, there were numerous photos of me in my white dress around the house, but that didn't stop her taking off her clothes and getting into my bed to be intimate with my man.'

Fay looks confused, so I go on.

'Logan doesn't know I'm aware of it yet, but I know he has cheated on me, and he cheated on me with this woman right here,' I say, pointing at the pathetic prisoner. 'I was out of the house, and he was home alone, or at least I thought he was. But I knew he had company when I got a notification on my phone to tell me that there had been movement detected on one of the cameras I have around our property. I have installed several secret cameras at this house and only I have access to the footage they record. Logan has no idea about them, and that is how I saw this woman at my front door and also how I saw my husband allowing her inside while I was several miles away running errands in town.'

I grind my teeth together for a moment, a bad habit that I picked up years ago and one that I always end up falling back into in moments of deep anger or stress. In this case, it is anger I am feeling as I recall the day that I discovered my husband being unfaithful to me.

'It's not just outside the house that I have secret cameras, but inside as well,' I go on. 'And that's how I saw Logan and this woman kissing before they undressed and fell into bed; the same bed I sleep in, I might add. This woman was a guest at the barn house, and she was supposed to be enjoying her stay in the lovely property I had built, but instead, she had taken advantage of seeing me leave and gone to pay my husband a visit in my absence. That made the whole thing worse as I stood there on the high street in town and watched this disgusting act on my phone. But once I knew about it, I had the chance to do something about it.'

'What the hell has this got to do with me?' Fay cries. 'Whatever sick game you're playing here, I don't want to be a part of it!'

'But you are part of it now, and so is Aidan, so shut up and let me finish,' I say, coldly.

Fay does not need the presence of the prisoner to make her realise that I am capable of doing bad things because she can clearly see that in my demeanour.

'Aware of what was going on in my home while I was out shopping, I added something extra to my shopping list that day. I picked up a bottle of something quite potent to humans if inhaled, and then I went home, though I waited until I saw this woman leaving my husband and going back to the barn. Then I kept quiet all night, acting as if everything was fine with Logan until he went to bed, no doubt feeling very smug and satisfied with his day's work while I had been out. But once he was asleep, I went to work, leaving the house and sneaking down to the barn. The lights were off inside, so confident the person inside was asleep, I snuck in.'

I smirk at my prisoner then, but all she can do is make more indecipherable noises while looking at Fay to help get her out of this mess. But Fay is looking at me, which tells me I finally have her full attention.

'It was easy to subdue her with a cloth soaked in chloroform because she was already asleep when I put it over her mouth and nose. Then, when she was out, I quickly tidied up all her things so that there was no trace of her left at the barn, then bundled her into the back of her car and drove her back to this house. While Logan slept upstairs, I carried her down here where he wouldn't find her. Then I drove her car out into the woods, set it alight and watched it burn before walking back. It was a very long night but so worth it.'

I smirk to myself when I think back on how I managed to achieve so much, fuelled simply by a desire for revenge and the adrenaline of knowing that I could get caught at any moment. From possessing the strength to drag Holly's unconscious body up and down stairs to walking back from where I ditched her car and only falling into bed around 4 am, it was a monumental effort. But it's funny what a woman can do when she is mad.

'She was due to check out the next day,' I explain further to the mortified Fay. 'But when we failed to see her, I went to the barn to check and when I did, I told Logan that she must have left. He might have been disappointed or probably just relieved but either way, he had no reason to think anything sinister had happened to her because some people left without saying goodbye, so it was not uncommon. She's been my prisoner ever since, and we've had a nice time together, haven't we?'

I wink at Holly and get her riled up even further, and it's then I notice that despite the feeble excuse for a meal I left her earlier, the plate on the floor beside her is empty, telling me she ate the cheese sandwich and was ultimately grateful for it.

'You're crazy,' Fay tells me then, and bless her, she probably thinks she is telling me something I don't know. 'How do you think you can get away with this? Somebody must know this poor woman is missing! How have the police not been here?'

'Sure, she's been reported missing in her hometown, which is four hours away from here,' I calmly reply. 'I've kept tabs on the local news there, and people are wondering where she went. But as far as they know, she just disappeared because like you when you came here, she paid cash, and she was looking for a complete escape from everyday life. Nobody knows she was here.'

I smile at Holly then, making sure my last few words there really resonated with her before I go on.

'But all good things must come to an end, and she can't stay down here forever, so it's time for her to go,' I say, and that seems to be the thing that gets Holly to become even more agitated.

'What are you going to do to her?' Fay asks me nervously, but I just shake my head.

'It's not what I am going to do to her, but what you are going to do to her for me.'

Fay has absolutely no idea what I am talking about, which is understandable, so I explain.

'You are going to kill this woman for me, and you are going to do it tonight. Otherwise, you will not leave this house alive and neither will your husband.'

Both Fay and Holly stare at me in stunned silence before Holly understandably starts to panic about what I've just said and has another go at trying to break free of her restraints.

'No. Are you kidding? I'm not killing her! I'm not being part of whatever this is!' Fay cries before she rushes at me again, and this time, despite my attempts to stop her, she forces her way past me and runs up the stairs. But I don't have to worry about that too much because the door always self-locks when it is closed, and only I have the key to open it, so Fay isn't going to get far.

I wait a moment while I allow her to figure that fact out for herself, and while she tries the door several times as well as calls out to Aidan, it doesn't do her much good. She's just as trapped as Holly is down here, but at least she has the chance to do something about it.

'As I said, Aidan needs you, and the only way you can help him is to do what I say and kill this woman for me,' I tell Fay calmly as I walk up the stairs towards her. But she is ignoring me and still busy trying the door handle, at least until I yank her arm behind her back and cause her to yelp out in pain.

'Careful, you don't want me to break your arm, do you?' I say as I easily lead Fay back down the stairs, her twisted limb bent back awkwardly out of position behind her as she keeps crying out in pain and begging me to let go. But I tell her I'll only do that if she does what I ask her to.

'I can't do it! I can't kill her!' Fay tries, but I'm not buying it.

'I think you can do whatever you need to do to protect yourself and your husband, so stop wasting time and do it now,' I say before I give her a big push and send her falling to the floor.

As Fay hits the ground and groans, I have one more thing to tell her about this basement that is full of surprises for her.

'There is a camera in here, so I can see what is going on at all times,' I tell her. 'There is also a knife in the drawer of the old cupboard in the corner. I suggest you use that, and I will be watching to see exactly what you do with it. If you do the right thing, then I will let you out of here, and you and Aidan can be together again, once he's woken up from his little nap, of course. But if you don't use that knife on her, then this door stays locked, and you'll never see Aidan ever again.'

With that said, I walk back up the stairs, and I only stop when I get to the door. Taking out the key, I look down on Fay lying by the bottom step and give her my final words.

'I'm just doing what I need to do. I trust you will do the same.'

With that, I put the key in the lock and open the door before quickly closing it behind myself.

I'm excited now to see what happens next on that camera in the basement.

But first, I better go and have a word with my husband.

# 14

## LOGAN

It was a big shock to see Aidan collapse right in front of me and fall onto the floor in the games room, but it was even more of a shock when I ran to get my wife so we could call an ambulance for help only to discover the letter she had left out for me on the coffee table in front of the fire.

My hands had been shaking as I had read the letter, no doubt as a result of the adrenaline caused from panicking about Aidan and the stress of whether or not he was dying in my house.

*But they started to shake even more when I read what was written on the page.*

I recognised Bridgette's handwriting immediately, so I knew she had been the one who had composed this message and as I read it, that only became more obvious.

***Dear Logan,***

***If you're reading this, it means you came to look for me and Fay after Aidan collapsed. Don't worry, he is not dead. He's just been drugged, but he will live, or at least he will as long as his wife does what I tell her to.***

***I will be with you shortly, but in the meantime, do not call for an ambulance or for the police. Trust me, you do not want to do that, or we will all end up in trouble.***

***I'll see you in a moment.***

***Bridgette***

The letter had confused the hell out of me before I ran back into the games room to check on Aidan's condition. But I found him in the same state that I'd left him in - unconscious but with a pulse and sat up against the wall, a position I had manoeuvred him into to try and make him somewhat more comfortable in his prone state.

*I'm still there with him when Bridgette reappears.*

'What the hell is going on?' I cry as I see my wife walk into the games room, looking remarkably calm considering the circumstances. 'What have you done?'

'Relax. Everything's okay,' my wife says, but she must be mad if she thinks that is true.

'What have you done to Aidan? We need to call for an ambulance,' I plead. 'What the hell is that letter all about? What the hell have you done?'

'I will tell you, but first, you need to calm down and follow me,' Bridgette says before she walks away, disappearing into the kitchen.

I feel uncomfortable leaving Aidan, but after checking his pulse again to make sure he is still with us, I have no choice but to follow my wife if I want to find out what this is all about.

Finding her in the kitchen, I see her standing beside a bottle of wine, but it's the small vial she holds up that she wants me to look at.

'I put this in Aidan's drink. That's why he's unconscious,' she tells me casually, as if it's not a totally insane thing to say. 'He'll wake up in a few hours and when he does, he'll have no idea what happened. He'll just think he drank too much and have a bit of a sore head, but other than that, there'll be no harm done.'

'No harm done? Are you kidding me? He collapsed, and the only reason he didn't bang his head on his way down was because I grabbed him before he hit the floor!'

'He'll be fine. Stop worrying about him,' Bridgette tells me, but she must be mad if she thinks I can just drop it.

'I'm calling an ambulance,' I say as I turn to go for the house phone, but Bridgette grabs my arm and holds me back.

'Don't be stupid! Do you want me to go to prison? And you'll go too. I'll tell them you were part of this!' she says, much to my disbelief.

'What?'

'Trust me. You do not want anybody to come here tonight. Not the paramedics, not the police, not anybody. If they do, then this is over for both of us, and this life we have here - this lovely life - will all go away. Do you understand me?'

I still have no idea what is going on, but I can tell that Bridgette is serious and that me calling 999 will not end well for any of us, so I do as she says and temporarily forget about making such a call. But I do need to do something. I need to sit down at the kitchen table and put my head in my hands because I am feeling overwhelmed.

'What have you done?' I mutter as I shake my throbbing head. 'Please just tell me.'

Bridgette takes a seat opposite me then before she produces her mobile phone and when she does, it looks like I am finally going to get some answers.

*The problem is, once I get them, I'm going to wish I was as oblivious as I was before.*

'Look here,' my wife tells me as she turns her phone to me to show me the screen. 'What do you see?'

It takes me a moment to figure out what I am looking at but once I have, I see two figures standing in a dimly lit room. It's a few seconds later when I realise that one of the women is Fay.

'What the hell? Where is she?' I say before figuring it out based on the noise I heard earlier. 'Is that our basement?'

'Yes, it is,' Bridgette tells me. 'But look more closely because it's not Fay whom I want you to focus on. It's the other woman. Do you recognise her? Come on, Logan. I know you do.'

I take a closer look at the grainy footage on the screen, but I'm still none the wiser as to who it could be. It's difficult to tell but I note she is tied to the wall, like some kind of prisoner.

*Who the hell is she?*

'I don't know,' I say. 'I can't see enough of her.'

'Keep looking,' Bridgette urges me sternly, evidently wanting me to figure this one out for myself, and that seems very ominous for me as I take another look.

And then I get it.

I know who this is.

*Bridgette can tell that I've just got it based on how pale my face must have just become.*

'That's right,' she says with a nod. 'It's Holly, the woman you cheated on me with.'

I let out what can only be called a nervous laugh as I stare at the screen and see that Bridgette is right. It is Holly, and she is the woman I cheated on my wife with.

*But I wasn't aware that Bridgette knew about that.*

'What's the matter? Just realised it's not quite the big secret you thought it was?' Bridgette says with a smirk. 'Sorry to have to tell you this, but you're not half as clever as you think you are, dear hubby. I saw Holly come inside this house while I was out, and I saw exactly what you did with her when she was in here.'

'How?' is the only thing I can say because we're clearly well beyond the point of me being able to say that I can explain this.

'Cameras,' Bridgette says swiftly. 'I have them all over the place, and they have got you into trouble, that's for sure. But not as much trouble as poor Holly is in. She's really in a tough spot right now, and as you can see here, there's not much she can do about it.'

I look around the room as if expecting to see a camera pointing right at me - one I've never noticed before - but I can't see anything, which is obviously the whole point of them being hidden. Then I look back at the phone screen and see that the two women in the footage are still not moving. They're just standing opposite each other; the only difference between them being that Fay seems to be free, whereas Holly is not.

'What is happening?' I ask nervously, wondering what twisted game my wife has decided to play. But it's a game that is far worse than I could ever have imagined when the rules are explained to me.

'Fay has to kill Holly for me,' Bridgette says chillingly. 'If she does that, then she can be with Aidan again.'

'Kill Holly? What are you talking about? You can't kill her!'

'Aren't you listening to me? I'm not going to kill her. Fay is. At least, she should do if she wants to get out of this herself. But that remains to be seen. All we can do is watch.'

'No, I'm putting a stop to this now!' I cry, and I get up from the table and go to leave the room, planning on kicking down that basement door if I have to, if that's what it takes to end this madness and free the two women trapped on the other side of it.

But just before I can do that, Bridgette speaks again and what she says causes me to stay where I am.

'I wouldn't go anywhere near that door if I was you,' she says coldly. 'If you do, then I will have no choice but to kill you.'

When I turn back around to look at my wife, that's when I see something even more frightening than what she just said to me.

I see that she means every word.

# 15

## FAY

The terrified woman tied up in front of me is still panicking, and that's not helping me think clearly. Trying to process the madness of this situation is hard enough without being so close to a prisoner who is desperate for me to help her. At least I assume that's what she is doing though it's impossible to hear her words with that handkerchief in her mouth. But I dare not remove it because the last thing I need is her begging for her life while I'm trying to think of the best way to save my own and Aidan's.

*Aidan.*

He's up there somewhere in the house, and he needs my help, and that's why I go running back to the basement door again to give the door handle another try. I already know it will be futile, but I have to give it a go, and as well as pulling on the handle, I'm kicking the door and shouting at the top of my voice for somebody to come and open it. But the door doesn't budge, nor do I get any word from anybody on the other side of it, and after wasting a couple of minutes, I turn away from the door and focus my attention on something else.

Bridgette told me there was a camera down here, so I go looking for it, and while it takes me some time, I eventually find it. The camera is high up in the far corner of the basement, directly opposite the corner in which the prisoner resides, which I guess gives Bridgette the best view of her whenever she wants to watch. But now I know where it is, I can give her something else to watch, and I walk towards the camera waving my arms above my head and shouting all manner of obscenities at the person on the other side of it. I also make sure to make plenty of rude gestures too, and while I know it's churlish of me to behave this way because it won't improve my situation much, it does feel good to let out some of my anger on the woman watching this basement like some sadistic voyeur behind an impenetrable barrier.

But despite getting all that off my chest, I give up when I see it is not getting us any closer to this door opening and either one of us being allowed out of here. That's when I have no choice but to turn back to the woman tied up behind me and think about engaging with her. But I remind myself that doing so might only make my task harder.

*The task in which I am supposed to kill this woman to save Aidan and, presumably, myself.*

Bridgette did not threaten me directly, but I would be stupid to think that this would end well for me if I did not do as she has asked. If she won't let Aidan go, then she won't let me go either, and that means she can get away with this if we're both dead. I have to get out of here, not only to save my husband, but to get revenge on Bridgette and Logan too because I assume he is in on this as well.

That's why I don't approach the woman yet.

*Instead, I approach the cupboard in the corner and slowly open the top drawer, the one in which Bridgette told me I would find a knife.*

Sure enough, there is a blade waiting for me in there, not that I am in any kind of a rush to pick it up. As I look down at it, I see it is the kind that one would expect to find in a kitchen, and even though it's still a very scary situation, I find a little comfort in that fact. It makes me feel less like Bridgette has been planning this for a long time, if it's just a knife she has taken from upstairs. Better that than something she has ordered online - a bigger blade designed for maximum impact.

But this knife is just as dangerous as any other one, I suppose, or at least it is in the wrong hands. But it's supposed to be in my hands and as I pick it up, the woman sees that it is now in my possession, and that only causes her to panic further.

I realise then that picking the knife up was a bad idea, so I drop it quickly back into the drawer and step away from it as if it can't do any damage to anybody if I keep my distance from it. But this isn't what I've been asked to do. I've not been told to avoid the knife. Rather, I've been told to use it to kill the woman I share this basement with.

*But can I?*

Going against my better judgement, I approach the fearful woman, and when I'm standing right in front of her, I speak quietly but clearly.

'We are going to talk. Okay?'

I wait for the woman to show me some sign that she has understood, and when she nods her head enthusiastically, I take that as her being okay with this plan, though she's still far from calm.

I decide that I am going to remove the handkerchief, which may be a mistake but how else am I going to be able to figure out what to do unless I speak to this woman and see if she has any ideas?

'Help me! Please!' the woman cries, her voice hoarse, no doubt due to a lack of water ever since she's been down here, but despite that, she tries to be as loud as she can.

'Untie me so we can get out of here!' she urges me, and while it would seem that would be the next logical step in me helping her, that is not what I'm supposed to be doing.

This woman heard Bridgette as well as I did.

I am supposed to kill her.

*But can I do it?*

'What's wrong? Help me!' the woman cries again, but I tell her to be quiet, and surprisingly, she does what I say. Then I get the chance to ask her a few questions.

'You slept with Logan?' I ask, seeking confirmation of what Bridgette told me.

'Yes, but I don't deserve this! Help me get out of here!' the woman cries, and I think she might have a point. Adultery does not usually lead to being locked up underneath a house to be slaughtered like some sacrificial lamb.

'Calm down,' I say, a stupid thing to tell a woman who is tied up because I know I would not calm down in her position. I would be begging for my life just like she is doing right here.

'Please. Don't do this,' she says desperately. 'I just want to go home. I won't say anything to anybody. I just want to get out of here, and then I'll stay away from you all, I promise.'

I don't doubt any of that for a second, but it's not as simple as that, and she must know it.

'Did you know Logan was married?' I ask her.

'What?'

'Did you know he was married when you slept with him?'

'I don't know. Who cares? I don't deserve this!'

'I care, so please tell me. Did you know he had a wife when you got into bed with him?'

The woman goes quiet for a moment before nodding her head.

'Yes, I knew,' she confirms.

'You saw his wedding ring?' I guess, but she shakes her head at that.

'No, I knew because I saw him with her when I checked in here.'

'You stayed at the barn house by yourself?' I ask, looking to get some clarification on the story Bridgette told me because I guess she could have been lying.

But the woman nods.

'So, you came here when you saw Bridgette go out and seduced Logan while she was away?' I ask, but she denies that vehemently.

'No, of course not. It wasn't as simple as that.'

'Then explain it to me,' I say before glancing back at the camera and wondering what Bridgette is making of my little chat with this woman. I presume the camera just captures live footage and not audio, which would mean that she can't hear what we are talking about down here, but I don't know for sure, so I am keeping my voice low just in case.

'I booked the barn house for a two-night stay,' the woman tells me quietly, clearly sheepish about what ended up happening, and who can blame her? 'I came here by myself because I'd just broken up with my boyfriend - my abusive boyfriend - and I needed some time on my own. I saw this barn house online and thought it sounded like the perfect place to get away from everything, so I called the owner and asked if I could come here. She said yes. I said I could pay in cash because I noticed there was a 20% discount if I did that, and then I arrived. I didn't tell anyone I was here because I didn't want my ex or anyone else knowing where I was. I planned on keeping myself to myself the whole time. But then I met Logan, and well…'

Her sentence drifts off then, but I urge her to carry on.

'Well, he's a good-looking guy, isn't he?' she says, and while I don't nod my head to agree, she takes my silence as agreement and carries on. 'He flirted a little with me as he showed me to the barn and helped me get settled in, and I admit I flirted back too. But that was all, and I didn't expect to see him again. Bridgette came by with a cake a little later, so I obviously figured they were a couple, but after that, I planned on staying inside the whole time on my own.'

'So how did you end up in his bed?' I ask her, cutting to the chase.

'Logan came down to the barn the second afternoon I was there,' she tells me. 'He asked if everything was alright and if I needed anything, but then he mentioned he was by himself. His wife had gone into town for the day, and he said he was a bit bored. He asked me if I was too. Said he often wondered how people kept themselves entertained in the barn with not much to do in there. I got the hint that he was keen for me to tell him I was just as bored as he was, but I didn't do anything straight away. I just thanked him for checking on me, and then he left.'

'Then what?'

She sighs then, but I remind her I don't have much more time for this story, so she goes on.

'I left it about half an hour before I walked up to the house,' she confesses.

'You went to have sex with him while his wife was out,' I confirm, but she doesn't want to say it was as simple as that.

'I don't know what I was doing,' she tells me. 'I'd been drinking wine, and I was messed up about my ex. I wasn't thinking straight. And the barn was so quiet. Too quiet. It started to drive me mad. I didn't plan it. If he hadn't come to see me, then I would never have gone there, and it would never have happened.'

'So, it's his fault?'

'No. Well, not entirely. It's my fault too.'

It's obvious that this woman takes her share of the blame for what happened.

'Then what?' I ask, wondering how she ended up down here.

'I felt guilty afterwards, so I went back to the barn and told Logan to stay away. I told him I was going to leave early in the morning so that I wouldn't have to see them, then I packed my things. I went to bed and set my alarm for 6 am, so I could be gone while they were both asleep in the house, and if Bridgette ever messaged me to ask why I'd left early, I'd just say something had come up, and I needed to go. But I don't know what happened after that.'

I try to imagine Bridgette sneaking into the barn while this woman slept, armed with both the chloroform and the knowledge that she had amassed from those secret cameras.

'I was asleep. I didn't hear her come to the barn. I didn't know how she did it,' the woman says desperately, but now we do.

'She drugged you,' I say solemnly.

'Yeah. The next thing I knew, I woke up in here, and I've been here ever since. I don't even know what day it is anymore. I have no idea how long I've been down here. Days? A week? My family will be so worried about me! You need to help me get out of here, please!'

That's when the woman starts panicking again, but while I tell her to calm down, she doesn't listen to me this time, and why would she?

She's just as desperate to get out of here as I am.

But can we do that?

*Or can only one of us escape this nightmare with our life intact?*

# 16

## BRIDGETTE

My partner knows what I'm like now, or rather, he knows about my crazy side. There are still several other things he doesn't yet know about me, but one thing at a time. I've already given him quite the shock this evening, so better to let him wrap his head around what I have already told him without giving him anything else to worry about.

Despite him threatening to leave the kitchen to go and kick down the basement door a moment ago, he has since re-joined me at the table, and I'm glad about that because it is in his best interests to have done so. Nothing good would have come from him trying to help the two women in the basement, and he knew that once I told him so.

Yes, the only reason he has sat back down with me again is because I threatened to kill him, but sometimes, a wife has to say whatever she can to get her husband to listen to her. I don't want to kill Logan, just like I don't want to kill anybody if I can help it. But it remains to be seen if I will come out of all this with my conscience clear or whether I will be joining the ranks of all the murderers out there, some of whom are currently in prison for their crimes but some of whom roam the streets, possibly having served their time and been released or more frighteningly, not yet having been found guilty of anything yet.

Of course, Logan does still have options here. He could run away with me and leave this house, just like he could defend himself if I tried to hurt him, and given that he is bigger and stronger than me, I'd say there was a good chance he would overpower me. But the very fact that I have even threatened him, mixed in with the state of shock he was in after seeing Aidan collapse and then finding out that not only did I know about his affair, but that the woman involved is locked in our basement, has rendered him almost useless. He's like a wounded animal - vulnerable and docile and in desperate need of somebody to look after him. The way I see it, I am the person to look after him, and I tell him that now.

'I can forgive you for what you did, but there has to be some form of payback,' I say to Logan while also keeping a close eye on my phone so I can see what is going on beneath us in that basement. 'Somebody has to pay for that illicit liaison, and seeing as how I don't want to lose you, it has to be her. You understand?'

Logan doesn't intimate that he does understand me, so I go on in the hopes that I can make myself clearer.

'If Holly dies, then I will feel much better about what you did with her,' I say confidently because I genuinely believe that. 'It will irritate me to know that she is walking around out there living her life and feeling sorry for who she thinks I am, which would presumably be a poor, naïve housewife who couldn't please her man. But that's not who I am, and I do not want her out there thinking that. I don't want her out there, full stop. I want her dead.'

'Then why don't you kill her then?' Logan snarls at me. 'If you want her dead so much, then you do it. Why drag Fay and Aidan into this?'

'Because I'm not a killer,' I say, stating what should be obvious, but I guess he needs reassuring on this point. 'I can't do it.'

'What makes you think Fay can do it?'

'The fact her husband's life depends on it, for one. And…'

There is something else I could say here to further strengthen my point, but I hold off saying it for the time being because mentioning it will only risk revealing one of the other secrets I have been keeping from my husband.

It's not just him who had things to hide.

I've got plenty as well.

*The only difference is I reveal my secrets when I'm ready, not when I get caught.*

'This is madness,' Logan says, shaking his head in disbelief. 'You've actually lost your mind. The fact that you would even have this idea is one thing, but to think that Fay is going to kill that woman just because you've told her to do so is ridiculous. You might hate Holly, but she doesn't, so she won't do it.'

'Are you sure about that?' I ask him, and when I turn my phone to Logan, he can now see what I have just seen, which is that Fay has opened the drawer and picked up the knife.

'You shouldn't underestimate her,' I tell my husband as he keeps watching, fearful of what might happen next. 'Just like you shouldn't underestimate me.'

We see Fay dropping the knife back down again then, and Logan seems to think that is proof that she won't go through with what I want her to do, but I just say it's normal for her to be reluctant and that this will take time.

'Patience,' I say to my husband as we watch Fay walking over to Holly, and a few moments later, she removes the prisoner's gag, so I guess the pair of them are talking now.

I can't hear what they are saying, but I can believe that Fay has just made a silly mistake. The more she gets to know the woman she is supposed to kill, the harder it will be for her to do that, and that's the reason I purposely did not give Fay Holly's name. I don't want her to personalise her and see this woman as anything more than just an obstacle in her way. Fay does not need to know Holly's name any more than she needs to know her age, background, family history and hopes for the future.

*All she needs to know is that the basement door does not get unlocked unless Holly is dead.*

Alas, for now, that woman is still alive, which is irritating, but I estimate it will be another hour or so until Aidan wakes up, so there's still plenty of time for Fay to do the deed. There's also plenty of time for Logan to raise a few more objections.

'I refuse to be a part of this,' he tells me, throwing his hands up and moving away from the phone as if no longer watching what is happening on it absolves him of all involvement, which, of course, it doesn't. 'What you have chosen to do here and what happens next is entirely on you, Bridgette. Do you hear me? I am not in on this with you, and I refuse to help you. I'm done.'

With that, Logan leaves the table, but I go after him, and when he sees me reaching for a knife on the kitchen counter, he immediately flinches.

'What are you doing with that?' he asks me, very afraid, which he should be because fear will help keep him alive.

'This?' I say, examining the sharp object in my hand. 'I was just going to go and cut some of that cheese in the lounge and have it on a cracker. Would you care to join me?'

Logan stares at me as if I've just said the strangest thing that he's ever heard a person say as I walk past him with the knife still in my hand. He moves out of my way as I go, not interested in getting any nearer to me and that blade than he already is, and I smirk to myself as I leave the kitchen and enter the lounge.

I find the cheeseboard where I left it, sitting on the table between the two sofas and in front of the fire, although the flames are petering out now, so I tell Logan to come and put another log on to keep it going. But he just stands uselessly in the doorway and watches me as I take a seat and cut into the cheese before taking a satisfying bite from the cracker I just put it on.

'Mmmm,' I say before reclining on the sofa and putting my feet up, and if he didn't know any better, Logan would think I was just enjoying a typical evening in our lovely home. But he does know better, much better, and that is why he is still too scared to do something as simple as put another log on the fire.

'Fine, I'll do it,' I say as I get up and walk over to the basket that we keep the wood pile in, and I pick up one of the many chunky logs we buy from the carpenter in town and toss it into the flames, watching it quickly be engulfed by the orange, swirling mass of heat.

'There, that's better,' I say with a smile before I make my way back to my seat and when I get there, I check on how things are going in the basement. When I do, I have another reason to smile.

That's because Fay appears to be holding the knife again.

*It looks like she is going to do as I say after all.*

# 17

## FAY

'What are you doing?'

That's a good question and while it was just asked by the woman tied up behind me, it's one I am also asking myself. That's because I've gone and picked up the knife again and while I am just holding it at the moment, I haven't decided what I am going to do next.

'I'm thinking,' I reply because that much is true.

'Thinking? What is there to think about? You just need to untie me so we can get out of here together!'

'Sssshhh,' I say, although that seems a little unlikely to work now that I've removed the mouth gag, and sure enough, I'm right.

'Hey! Come on! We're on the same side here! Let's help each other!' the woman I'm supposed to kill tells me, and I want to shut her up somehow, but as I approach with the knife, she starts to panic, presuming this is the end for her.

'Get away from me! No, don't do it!' she cries until I put the knife down again and tell her I'm not going to stab her, at least not yet anyway, though I don't mention that last part.

'Calm down. I just need you to be quiet because I need to think and you're distracting me,' I say, but that seems to be the green light for this woman to try and confuse me even more because she suddenly starts rambling about everything.

'My name is Holly! I am twenty-eight, and I work as a nurse at Charring Hospital! My mum and dad's names are Ida and Glenn, and I have two brothers, Max and Charlie! We spend every Christmas together, and Charlie is due to get married next year!'

'Why the hell are you telling me this?' I ask, but I already know the answer. Holly, as I now know she is called, is aware that the more I know about her, the harder it will be for me to kill her, so that's why I'm getting the whole spiel about her family.

'Max has a dog called Baxter, and he got sick once when he was small. I was looking after him that day, so I took him to the vets and sat with him all day until they fixed his leg and he was allowed to go home. I thought he was going to die, but he was okay, and now he's old, but he's still just as adorable.'

'Shut up!'

'No, I will not! I have a family who loves me, and they want to see me again! I have friends too! My best friend is called Kelly, and we met in primary school. We've been best friends ever since, and she lives around the corner from me! She's getting married soon as well, and I'm the chief bridesmaid! I was organizing things for her hen party before I came here. We're going to Barcelona! There's twelve of us, including her mum, who is called Pamela and is like a second mother to me!'

I reach out for the gag and go to stuff it into Holly's mouth because I've heard far too much and don't wish to hear another word about this woman and all the people who will miss her if she's gone. But just before I can silence her again, she has one more thing to say.

'I have a daughter!'

I freeze when I hear her say that.

'What?'

'That's right. I have a daughter. She's called Katy!'

I really wish I hadn't just heard what I've heard because there is no doubt that makes this even harder. *Holly is a mother?*

'Wait, why didn't you mention that first?' I ask her, suddenly sceptical. 'Why did you talk about your parents and your brothers and your friends, even a damn dog, all before you mentioned you have a child?'

I'm wondering now if Holly has just made up the fact that she is a mum and if so, what else could she be lying about? Some of what she has told me? All of it? If I can't trust her, then all I can do is trust Bridgette, who says she will kill Aidan if I don't do as she says.

'Because I'm ashamed,' Holly says, which was not the answer I was expecting.

'What?' I ask, my hand still on the fabric of the mouth gag, but so far, I have not put it back over her mouth.

'I'm ashamed,' Holly repeats, and I notice a tear sliding down her cheek below her left eye then.

'Ashamed? Of what?'

'Of leaving her when she needed me.'

'What are you talking about?'

'I left my daughter when she was small,' Holly confesses, the tears coming quicker now. 'I was only young when I had her, and I couldn't cope, so I left her. I ran away and left her with the father.'

'You ran away,' I repeat, wondering how she could do that, but she has given me a reason already. She was young and couldn't manage the responsibility, and judging by how much she is crying now, I'd say she has regretted it ever since.

'It was the biggest mistake of my life,' she tells me in between sobs. 'I missed the entire first year she was alive before I got back in touch with the father. But he hated me and still does, but he has allowed me to spend some time with her. I'll never be able to be a full-time mum to Katy, but I've been trying, I really have. She's nearly ten and will be starting secondary school soon. She's beautiful - she really is - much prettier than me, and smarter too. I love her so much, and I'd do anything for her.'

Holly's sob story is not doing anything to help my cause, and I go to stuff the handkerchief back in again, but she keeps going.

'Please, I can't leave her again! I left her once, but I can't do it again! If you kill me, then she'll never know what happened, and she'll think I just ran away like I did before! But I would never leave her, not after last time! Please, don't let her spend the rest of her life thinking her mother didn't love her!'

I think about what Holly has just said for ten seconds or so. While I try and do that, looking from the camera to the knife to the wriggling woman tied up, I still feel like I have absolutely no idea what to do.

I guess I could try the door again, but what will that accomplish? I can't open it - only Bridgette can - and she won't do that unless she sees me kill Holly on camera.

I stare into that camera for several long seconds, hoping my eyes are boring into the woman on the other side of it and that she is feeling my anger and sense of injustice. She's left me in an impossible situation, and I want her to know it. Either I kill Holly and leave Katy motherless or I do nothing and let Aidan die upstairs.

What do I do?

*I better decide very soon because the longer this goes on, the less likely this is to end well for me.*

I pace around the basement for several minutes, running through every scenario and eventuality in my head, but all that does is leave me even more confused. That's when I stop walking and stare back at the camera.

Then I make my decision.

Reaching down to pick the knife up off the floor, I turn to Holly and give her a sad shake of the head. Then I approach her, the knife out in front of me and the blade getting closer to the stricken woman by the second.

She's trying to speak, but I can't hear her, and only her eyes can do the talking for her now. They are eyes that tell me everything I need to know.

She is afraid and she does not want to die.

But as I reach her, the knife still out in front of me and ready to penetrate whatever it can come into contact with, I only have two words to say to Holly now.

'I'm sorry.'

# 18

## BRIDGETTE

Needless to say, neither myself nor Logan uttered a single word as we watched Fay stab Holly in the basement. We both just stared at my phone screen in stunned silence as we watched the blade go into her lower abdomen before Holly's head hung down, and she slumped to the floor before Fay stepped away from her body and walked up the stairs to the door. That's where she remains now, the woman who just killed for me, although I better not leave her waiting there too long because she has just done as I asked, so she deserves to be rewarded for that.

'Bravo,' I say as I clap my hands together twice now that the deed is done and that bitch is dead. I can't say there was ever a time when I was completely certain that Fay would do what I had asked of her, but I always knew there was a good chance considering the pressure I had put her under. Now it seems she has risen to the occasion and done what she had to do to save her husband, and that is why it is time to unlock that basement door.

'I guess I better go and let her out,' I say as I stand up, but Logan grabs my arm before I can go any further, holding me tightly, his hand feeling cold, just like the stare he is giving me as I look down at him.

'What are you doing?' he asks me as if I haven't just already told him.

'I'm going to open the door and let her out.'

'Are you serious? She has a knife, and she's just killed Holly. What's to say she won't try and kill us too?'

I appreciate that it's a valid point worth raising, but I don't harbour any of my husband's fears.

'She won't do that,' I tell him, trying to reassure him, though it will likely take more than me giving him my word for it after what he has just witnessed.

I can already see the effect that Holly's demise has had on him because he looks terrified but not just because he worries that he might be next. It's because he knows that woman died because of him, and even if he does get out of this alive, he's going to have to live with that fact for the rest of his days, and that is a burden that will be impossible to shed. But I'm not going to feel sorry for him because he has brought this on himself. All he had to do was be faithful to me and this wouldn't have happened.

*All actions have consequences, dear.*

'How do you know she won't try and hurt us?' he asks me, still gripping my arm.

'Let go of me. It will be fine.'

'How can you be so sure?'

'Well, what do you suggest? We leave her in the basement forever? That means we'd kill her, and I suppose we'd have to kill Aidan then as well. Are you willing to do that?'

'No, of course not.'

'Then I have to open that door.'

I pull away from Logan's grasp then because he is wasting my time with his worries, but as I approach the basement door, I realise I should take some precautions before I unlock it. That's why I lean in closely to the door and speak to Fay through it.

'I'm going to let you out now, but you need to slide the knife under the door first,' I tell her before I step back and look down.

A moment later, I see a bloodied knife appear from beneath the door, and the sight of the strong red colour on the silver blade is quite unsettling. But it is also proof that Fay has done what I asked of her, so without further ado, and after picking up the knife, I turn the key and allow her out.

As the door opens, I step back because I have no idea what kind of Fay I will be getting. A quiet, contemplative one? Or an angry, vengeful one? I keep hold of the knife until I know for sure, but it seems it is the former because Fay says nothing as she walks out of the basement until the door has been closed behind her. Then she simply asks me where Aidan is.

She is struggling to make eye contact with me, and I can see just how much the experience in the basement has taken out of her, but rather her than me because if I'd killed Holly, then I'd be the one wrestling with all that guilt now. As it is, I feel fantastic and not at all upset about that woman and what happened to her, nor for Fay and what she is going through now, too.

'This way,' I say to her before I call out for Logan to come and help us, something he is very reluctant to do, although he looks a little better when he sees that Fay no longer has the knife.

The three of us enter the games room, and when Fay spots Aidan slumped on the floor against the wall, she rushes over to him and checks for a pulse.

'He's fine,' I tell her, but she has to check for herself anyway and only once she knows that is true does she relax a little. But only a little.

'When will he wake up?' she asks me.

'Within the next hour or so,' I reply. 'We should put him somewhere comfortable for when he does. We'll take him down to the barn house and put him into bed. When he wakes up, you'll just tell him that he got a little woozy after a couple more glasses of wine and we decided to call it a night. He'll just think he drank too much.'

'That's it?' Fay says curtly. 'You've drugged him and made me stab a poor woman, and now you just expect us to go back to the barn and get into bed. Go to sleep? Wake up in the morning and check out like everything is normal and we haven't just had the craziest night of our lives? I don't think so. You are going to help me put Aidan in the car because we are getting out of here right now.'

'I wouldn't do that if I was you,' I advise her. 'If Aidan wakes up in the car and finds out you have left the barn suddenly, he will have a lot more questions than if he wakes up in bed and just figures he overindulged a little bit. What would you say to him then?'

'I'll tell him the truth,' Fay hisses. 'I'll tell him that you two crazy psychos drugged him, and then you made me stab a woman in your basement!'

'Hey, I did not drug anybody!' Logan cries, and Fay looks puzzled by that, as well she might because she must assume that the pair of us are in on this together. But that's not the most important thing to discuss.

'And then what will you do?' I ask Fay with a smirk on my face. 'Go to the police? Tell them you've killed somebody. I'm sure they will be very interested to hear that. You can tell them you did it under duress all you want, but it won't change the fact that you plunged that knife into Holly and took her life. You'll serve time for that. Serious time. Could you cope in prison, Fay? Could you handle being behind bars for the next several years? You won't see much of Aidan. Maybe he'll meet somebody else and move on. But that will be the least of your problems. You'll have enough to worry about trying to keep yourself safe from the other inmates, people who didn't kill because they were forced to but killed because they wanted to and enjoyed doing so. Good luck surviving amongst them.'

'I didn't say anything about the police, did I?' Fay remarks as she stands up again and momentarily leaves Aidan alone in order to fix all her attention on me. 'Maybe we'll just come back and get revenge on you? Have you considered that?'

I laugh then to let Fay know that not only have I considered it, but I have done so and then deemed it something I don't need to worry about.

'You won't be coming back here, and you know it,' I say with a satisfied smile. 'Once you've left here, you'll never look back because you know what's good for you, or at least I hope you do. All you are going to do is run away and get on with the rest of your lives, and you will never mention what happened here tonight to anybody for as long as you live because you don't want to get into trouble. Isn't that right?'

I study Fay's defeated expression and take great satisfaction in it before I reiterate what is going to happen next.

'We're going to take Aidan to the barn, and then your involvement in this will be over,' I tell Fay. 'Then you'll leave as planned in the morning and be on your way. After that, we'll never see each other again. Now, let's move him before he wakes up.'

With that, I take hold of one of Aidan's legs before looking to Fay and Logan to help me.

And guess what?

They both do.

# 19

## LOGAN

There are so many crazy things that have happened tonight that helping my wife and a killer put an unconscious man into the back of my car is not even the weirdest of them all.

It was hard work getting Aidan out of the games room and into the trunk of my vehicle, but the three of us managed it between us and now he's in, I can drive him down to the barn before we have to take him out and carry him again.

Bridgette says she will accompany Fay down to the barn while I drive, and as I get in behind the wheel and start the engine, the headlights from the car land on the two women walking away into the darkness.

If I didn't have a drugged man with me, then I would be seriously tempted to just turn around and drive away from here, if only to get some space from all this insanity. But rather than risk encountering a police officer out on the country lanes who might ask me what I'm doing, I decide to stay here and just do as Bridgette says.

That seems to be the only play here. Do what my wife says. Fay has certainly done that and because she has, she seems to now have the chance to come out of this safely.

*So I guess I'll try for the same.*

Releasing the handbrake and gently pressing the accelerator, I put the car into motion and move slowly down the track towards the barn, staying behind the pair of walking women who I can still see through my windscreen. They don't appear to be talking, but maybe that's to be expected. There can't be much call for small talk after what they have done this evening.

Maybe I'm still in shock, or maybe I'm simply terrified of both these women and what they are capable of, but whatever it is, I intend on keeping myself to myself now and just getting this over with as quickly as possible. As I park outside the barn and turn the engine off, I get the sense Fay has made the same plan because she says nothing, simply taking hold of Aidan along with Bridgette, and when I join them, the three of us work as a team once again to get Aidan to where he needs to be.

It's extremely hard work getting the man up the stairs, and I'm sweating profusely by the time we manage to lay him down on the bed. I'm amazed he hasn't woken up yet with all the moving around he's been forced into doing, but Bridgette seemed very confident about how long the drugs she gave him would knock him out for, and I have no reason to doubt her because she has been right about everything else so far.

It's terrifying to think how she has been one step ahead of all of us tonight. She knew exactly what she was doing when she invited this couple to our house, just like she knew when she handed Aidan his particular glass of wine and later when she took Fay down into the basement where she gave her the grim task. And she was well ahead of me too, aware of my affair almost as soon as it happened, and despite me thinking I'd got away with it, I was merely living in a dream state in which naivety was my only friend.

'Right, time to go,' Bridgette tells me once Aidan is where she wants him to be, and we both turn to the stairs. But before we go, Fay has one more thing to say.

'You won't get away with what you have done,' she says, more to Bridgette than me, which I appreciate even if it is still a chilling message all the same.

But does my wife seem troubled by this dramatic statement?

*Not in the slightest.*

'We will both get away with what we have done, and that will be the end of it,' she says calmly. 'You have just as much to lose as I do, if not more, so you will stick to the plan, and we will say nothing else on the matter. Now, goodnight, Fay, and thank you for staying with us. I recall that you needed to leave early in the morning, so you carry on and do that. Please leave the key on the table, and if you do get a minute, don't forget to write a review in the guest book.'

With that, my unbelievably bold wife walks down the stairs, and rather than stay here and have a very uncomfortable moment with Fay, I decide to quickly follow her so I can leave this barn too.

Once outside, Bridgette gets into the passenger seat of the car, and I guess we're driving back to her house together. It's a short journey we make in silence, although it's not because I am lacking for something to say. In fact, there is one very important topic I wish to discuss with my wife, and it is an almighty elephant in the room, or should that be car.

*It's the issue of what to do with Holly's body in the basement.*

The only thing keeping me from asking Bridgette what the plan is there is fear. I'm afraid because I don't want to get confirmation that I am supposed to help her dispose of it. I know the body can't stay in our basement forever and that it has to be buried somewhere, but I do not wish to be a part of that. Bridgette will have to do that herself, although I'm not sure how she would manage that. But it's not my problem. It's hers.

Yeah, right.

*I really wish I could believe that.*

I park back at the house, and we get out of the car without a single word still having been spoken between us since we left the barn. I follow Bridgette inside then, but I'm walking slowly as if my body knows to be wary because every step I take is bringing me closer and closer to the body that resides here.

Will Bridgette mention it now that we are back inside with the front door closed? Will she tell me what her plan is? Will she instruct me to get one of the big suitcases down from the attic because we are going to bundle Holly's body into one of those and then drive her to the coast and throw the case into the sea? Or will she tell me to go to the garage and get my tools because we are actually going to cut Holly up into little pieces so it will be easier to move her?

Whatever she is about to say, I hold my breath as my wife stops walking ahead of me and turns to face me before finally broaching the terrible subject I have been waiting for her to bring up.

'You invited Holly into this house, so you can get her out of it,' she says coldly. 'I'm going to bed now. Goodnight.'

Bridgette heads for the stairs then, leaving me staring at her in disbelief. Does she really think she can just end the night on that note? If so, she can think again.

'Wait! Where do you think you're going? I'm not moving Holly. You wanted her dead, so you can deal with her body!' I say, feeling well within my rights to make such a point. 'You're lucky I haven't called the police yet and had them come here to arrest you and Fay for what you've done.'

'I'm lucky?' Bridgette says, stopping suddenly and turning back to me, and when I see the look on her face, I almost wish she hadn't. 'My husband cheated on me in my own home. Please explain it to me because I can't quite see it. How am I lucky?'

'Oh, come off it,' I say, incredulous. 'Okay, I cheated, and it was wrong! Then go ahead and divorce me like a normal wife would! But you couldn't be normal, could you? You've helped to kill that poor woman, and now you expect me to do the rest of your dirty work for you? It's not happening. Not a chance.'

I am the one to walk away then, going into the kitchen to get myself a very strong drink. But I don't hear Bridgette follow me, which is a good and a bad thing. It's good because it means we don't have to carry on this argument, and I can have a much-needed minute to myself. But it's bad because that body in the basement is still very much an unresolved issue, and the longer it lingers there, the more chance there is of us getting caught with it in our house. But the drink is my first concern, and after pouring a very large measure from a bottle of whiskey I have been slowly but surely working my way through over the last several weekends, I head into the lounge area where I find the fire has died out. Sadly, it is not the only thing that has died in this house tonight, and as I notice Bridgette's phone lying on the sofa, I see that the screen is still showing footage of the basement. But as I look more closely, I see there is a problem and it's not the one I was expecting to see.

I should be looking at Holly's body lying on the ground.

*But when I look, I can't see it anywhere.*

I am very confused because I know for sure that I saw Holly fall down and lie motionless on the ground when Fay stabbed her, and I also saw the bloodied knife that Bridgette was carrying, proving that Holly had indeed been stabbed.

So where is she now?

I leave the lounge and walk through the hallway, thinking about calling out to my wife upstairs. But not only do I not want to see her again so soon after we just parted, but I tell myself there is nothing strange going on here. Holly will still be in the basement because not only can she not get out, but she was wounded, supposedly mortally so, so even if she has crawled across the floor and out of view of the camera, she can't have got very far.

Stopping in front of the basement door, I listen for a moment but hear nothing on the other side of it. But I won't know for sure that Holly is really dead in there unless I go in and have a look, and when I see the key still sitting in the lock, I know that all I have to do is turn it, and I will get my answer.

So that's what I do.

I turn the key, and I open the door.

When I do, I get the shock of my life.

*Holly is standing right in front of me - covered in blood but very much alive.*

Is she a ghost? An apparition? A demon back from the dead?

I have absolutely no idea because the next thing I know, I've fallen to the ground, the combination of shock, light-headedness and a severe tightness in my chest leaving me utterly useless.

And as I lie there and drift into unconsciousness, I see Holly's feet walking away from me.

# 20

## FAY

I've been trying to wake Aidan up ever since Bridgette and Logan helped bring him back to this barn, but so far, I have been unsuccessful. Whatever drug that bitch gave him really knocked him out cold. But I have to keep trying to wake him because, based on what I've done, I know time is of the essence, and it won't be long until that couple find out that I have not killed Holly after all.

*At least, I hope I haven't.*

I stabbed her because it had to look real on camera, and I needed the knife to be covered in blood when I left the basement and showed it to Bridgette, but that doesn't mean I want Holly to have died. I'm hoping she has survived her injuries because if not, I have killed her, and I'll have to live with that. But there's a chance she's okay and if so, she can escape this place too, and that's only because I decided to give her that chance.

As much as I did not want to harm Holly, I knew there was no way out of that basement for either of us unless it genuinely looked like I had stabbed her to death. The knife had to penetrate her body; she had to collapse to the floor, and there had to be blood. There was simply no other way to try and fool those watching on camera. But after Holly had told me she was a nurse during her desperate rant in which she informed me about who she was and who would miss her, I had an idea. At first, I didn't think it would work, so I had prepared myself to do what Bridgette had asked, and I guess I was going to kill her but only because Aidan's and my life depended on it too. But as I had the knife ready to strike, I paused for a second before asking Holly where the best place to stab her on her abdomen was. I wanted her to live, so I needed to avoid all the vital organs, and while I knew it wasn't guaranteed and wouldn't be perfect, I had to at least try and give her a shot at getting out of here.

The knife had to hurt her.

*But maybe we could limit the damage it did.*

Whispering in case there was a chance Bridgette was trying to listen in, Holly told me that she might survive if I pierced one of her kidneys, and while she would bleed heavily, with luck, she could live as long as she got medical attention in the next few hours. But even aiming for a 'safer' spot, there was still a chance of me getting it wrong and hitting something crucial like an artery or a more dangerous organ, although it was sadly a chance I would have to take. I could hardly stab her in the leg or arm and make it look entirely convincing. It had to be her torso because that's where any normal person would look to stab if they had to, so once I had my target area defined, I went for it, though Holly was still desperate for me to come up with another plan.

*But I just ignored her because there was no other way.*

It felt awful to feel the knife entering Holly's skin, and I was almost sick as I saw the first signs of blood. I wanted to close my eyes but had to keep them open to make sure I was piercing the 'right' area and because of that, I saw Holly's eyes go wide in pain before she let out an awful groan that I'm sure will stay with me for a long time. But while the knife had gone in, I also knew once might not be convincing, so I forced myself to strike one more time, though this blow was more of a slash across her stomach rather than a deep, penetrating plunge, although I'm sure it looked damn convincing on camera.

*I bet it looked even more convincing when Holly collapsed to the floor and didn't move.*

Aware of my audience, I had bent down then to check for a pulse and been hugely relieved when I had still felt one, although it had been alarming to see just how much blood was leaking out of Holly's body, and I feared I'd already done far too much damage. But it was all about the performance, and if it felt real down in the basement, then it had to feel real for those watching from outside of it.

The last thing I did while I was making it seem like I was checking for a pulse was cut through the rope that held Holly to the wall. Her arm was hanging up awkwardly where she was still tied, so I allowed it down so her body could rest easier on the floor. It was a thing that, to Bridgette, would have seemed more like a final act of respect to the deceased, but really, it was an act that was actually going to give Holly a chance of getting out of there while everyone thought she was already dead.

But has she done it? Is she out of that basement now, or has she succumbed to her wounds? And have Bridgette and Logan realised she isn't dead after all? If it's the latter, what does that mean for not only Holly, but for me and Aidan too?

'Wake up, damn it!' I say as I shake Aidan again before giving him a slap across the face for good measure. But it's no good. He still doesn't stir, and I guess Bridgette was right. It will be an hour or so before he does wake up.

*But I might not have that much time.*

I note how peaceful my partner looks as he lies here before me, and even though he has been drugged, I can't help but feel envious of him for a second because while he's been out cold, I've been through hell. He's been sleeping while I've been locked up in a basement and given an awful ultimatum, and since he was last awake, I've stabbed a person. That's why I'm jealous of him. He has no idea what he has missed, but if he's not careful, he will never know because he might not get the chance to wake up again if that couple come back here with bad intentions.

Getting off the bed and leaving my unconscious husband in peace for a moment, I make my way over to the window and tentatively peel back one of the curtains, anxious to see outside and, more specifically, if anybody is coming to this barn. In my paranoid state, I almost expect to see both Bridgette and Logan marching towards me like some angry villagers in one of those movies - the kind where they carry flame torches and pitch forks and have furious expressions on their faces. But mercifully, for now anyway, there is no sign of anybody coming to the barn, so I guess that means they haven't found out that I've lied to them yet.

Is that a good thing or a bad thing?

Surely they went to check on Holly when they got back to the house. If they think she is still dead, then maybe she is. Or maybe they are busy finishing her off now, having temporarily been stunned to find her alive only to finish what I should have done half an hour ago. *Once they're done killing her, then I guess they'll be on their way down here to kill us.*

With that last thought still prominent in my mind, I consider my options. Ideally, I would get Aidan and myself out of here as quickly as possible, but that's not possible with my husband being nothing more than a dead weight at this moment in time. There's no way I can get him into our car by myself so I can drive us away. I'd need him to move his own body, but he can't do that until he's conscious again. I knew that, which is why I told Bridgette that we would just leave tonight, hoping that she and Logan would settle for putting Aidan into the car and allowing us to be on our way. But they did not allow that, and now I'm stuck here.

If I can't leave until Aidan wakes up, then the only other thing I can do is try to defend myself, and that is why I'm now going downstairs to the kitchen to find a weapon. But the knives in the cutlery drawer are not particularly sharp, presumably how Bridgette wanted it, so they aren't much good. In the end, I guess the best thing I have is a corkscrew and while it's hardly an unbeatable weapon, I keep it in my hand as I walk around the barn and check out of the other windows.

It's still dark and quiet out there, but I know it's not going to last that way.

Bridgette will come back here soon; I just know it.

*When she does, I better be ready for her.*

# 21

## BRIDGETTE

One might think that it would be difficult to sleep after everything that's happened tonight, but I have a feeling I will slip into a slumber just fine. That's because for the first time since my husband cheated on me, I will be able to lay my head down on my pillow in the knowledge that the woman he strayed with is now gone for good, and she paid the ultimate price for her sins.

I'm in my bedroom and preparing to undress, having come straight up here after getting back from the barn. I was tempted to go and look at Holly's corpse in the basement, but I decided that I would be making far more of a point to Logan if I told him that he was to deal with her now. My line about him being responsible for inviting her into this house so he was responsible for getting her out of it was a stroke of genius, if I do say so myself, and it would have had far less impact if I had gone to the basement with him.

Leaving him to clean up the mess he started is the best way for him to truly learn this harshest of lessons that I have tried to teach him tonight, and that lesson is this:

*You do not mess with me.*

I take out my earrings and start to clean off my make-up, smiling at myself in the mirror on my dressing table as I do because I am satisfied with what has been accomplished here this evening. I almost couldn't have expected the plan to go so well when I first conceived of

it, but everything has gone off without a hitch, and I guess I should have had more confidence in myself.
I suppose the reason for my nervousness was because it's been a very long time since I did anything half as dastardly as this. There was a time when I was fully immersed in a life of crime, but that was a very long time ago before I met Logan and transformed myself into a supposedly normal member of society, and it's a part of my past still unbeknownst to my husband to this day. I became just another wealthy man's wife when we wed, or at least I did to the outside world. But I have never truly lost connection with my roots; the real me, the me who is good at certain things that the rest of society deem unacceptable, and I guess I never will.

I'm interrupted then by a bang downstairs and while I'm not sure what it was, I pause for a moment to see if I hear it again. I don't, but curiosity has me now, so I call out to Logan to ask him what it was.

*But I get no answer.*

I assume it was something to do with him moving Holly's body, or maybe he has just got frustrated and punched a wall after having a drink. I'd be angry too, if I was him. But I still don't know for sure, so I call out to him again, and when he fails to answer me for a second time, I leave the bedroom to go and investigate.

'Logan?'

One more attempt at communicating with my husband yields no response and while he could just be mad at me and choosing to ignore me, I have to know for sure, so I'm about to go downstairs to try and find him. But just before I do, I look over the banister to see the hallway beneath me and when I do, I get a nasty surprise.

*I see my husband lying on his back with his eyes closed and his hand over his chest.*

'Logan!'

I'm running down the stairs now, desperate to check on him and find out if he is still breathing and when I reach him, I get my answer.

*But it is not the one I wanted.*

I detect no signs of breathing, nor does it seem possible to wake him up. The next thing to do is check for a pulse and while I initially feel relief when I detect one, I suddenly have the awful realisation that what I am feeling is actually the pulse from my finger after the exertion of running down the stairs. When I check again and allow a little more time to really differentiate between my pulse and a potential one from my husband, I realise there is a big difference.

My heart is still beating.

*But his is not.*

'Oh no,' I say as I try to figure out what happened here, but the fact Logan appears to be clutching his chest gives me a clue. I think he's had a heart attack, and given he had to go for a check-up last year after being diagnosed with high blood pressure, I already knew his heart was not in the greatest of health. But I didn't realise he was in danger of dropping dead at any moment, although it doesn't take me long to see that the events of tonight most likely played a big part in triggering this.

All the stress and shock of what I've done with Holly, Aidan and Fay must have contributed to him keeling over and succumbing to a deadly heart attack. It can't be a coincidence that he has collapsed tonight, of all nights.

I have caused this, and now my husband is dead.

My cheating husband but still, he was mine.

*But now he's gone.*

As I shed a tear and try to process this, I remember there is something else that is now my problem too. I'd told Logan to deal with the body in the basement, but now he's gone, I guess that responsibility is going to fall on me.

It must have been the shock of seeing my husband in such a prone position that caused me not to notice the open door in front of him, but as I turn and look at it, I see the basement door is wide open and figure he must have been on his way in there when he had the attack.

Staring into the dark void that is the basement, I think about what is waiting for me when I go in there. The bloodied body of a woman I loathed, presumably. But what should I deal with first?

Her or him?

With Logan having only recently passed, I know I shouldn't leave it too long before I call 999 and request the emergency services. They'll be far too late to do anything when they arrive - I already know that - but a normal person would call them as soon as possible, so I better try and act normal here. But that means Holly's body will still be in this house when the paramedics arrive, and that makes me very nervous. But what else can I do? I can't waste time trying to move Holly, can I? People might get suspicious if they can tell I didn't call for help for my husband for several hours after he died. Then again, I was upstairs getting ready for bed. I could just tell them that I was having an early night and went up to bed ahead of my husband, falling asleep while he was still downstairs enjoying his evening. That would give me a plausible excuse as to why I waited so long to call the ambulance. I'll tell them that I had no idea my husband had died until I woke up in the morning and realised he had never come to bed.

I take a deep breath and realise I probably have more time than I first thought to decide what to do next, so I figure it is best not to rush and do something hasty that I might later regret. I've been calculated so far, so why change now?

Slowly stepping through the basement doorway, I turn on the light inside and prepare to look at my second dead body of the evening. But at least this one won't upset me as much as seeing my husband did.

As I walk down the stairs, I brace myself for the blood because there was plenty on the knife, so there should be even more down here. I also wonder if Holly's eyes will be open or shut, hoping for the latter because that will be a little less startling.

But nothing can prepare me for how startled I am when I see that the basement is empty.

Holly is not here.

She's not lying on the ground covered in blood.

That must mean she is not dead.

*But if she's alive, where is she?*

# 22

## AIDAN

The first thing I hear when I wake up is my wife's voice, loud and clear in my left ear as if she is shouting into it, though I have no idea why.

The noise is almost deafening, and she's giving me an almighty headache, although I would soon come to discover that my crippling headache had less to do with her and more to do with another woman. But as I struggle to regain my senses, the first thing I see is a ceiling I don't recognise, before Fay's face appears, staring down at me before she slaps me on the face, not hard but just enough to give me a jolt and wake me up even more.

That's when I feel like I'm going to be sick.

'Urgh,' I moan as I try to make sense of where I am and what has happened to me. I feel like I've had the heaviest of nights, the kind I used to experience when I was younger and would stay up until dawn drinking all sorts of strong spirits that made me feel invincible when I was drinking them but ultimately, left me feeling like I was dying once I stopped and sobered up. But even in my youth, I don't ever recall waking up feeling as bad as this, nor do I ever remember waking up to my wife slapping me in the face and shouting my name.

*What is she doing?*

'Aidan! Come on! We need to leave!'

Fay is still making a lot of noise, but she is not making much sense, and I try to tell her that, but when I go to speak, my throat is incredibly dry and the words catch in it. It's then I realise that I am lying on a bed, though I have absolutely no idea how I got here because the last thing I remember, I was playing pool with Logan.

But for some reason, I'm back in the barn with no memory of how I got here.

*What happened?*

'Water,' I gasp as I close my eyes again and try to ease my throbbing headache, and when Fay hands me a cup, I gulp down everything inside it, relieving my throat, but it's about the only relief I get because I still feel terrible.

'What happened?' I ask Fay as I hand her back the empty cup. 'How did I get here?'

Fay replies then, but I haven't heard her correctly because I thought she said the word 'drugged'. But I must have misheard her, right?

'What?'

'You were drugged by Bridgette. She put something in your wine, and you passed out.'

Fay is still not making any sense, but the room feels like it's spinning now, so that is my main concern. Rolling over onto my side, I take several deep breaths and as I do, I wonder if I simply drank too much alcohol with Bridgette and Logan and got myself into this state. Maybe Fay is talking about me being drugged because I might have told her that as an excuse as she helped me to bed when I was wasted. I must have been so embarrassed that I said Bridgette put something in my wine.

That makes more sense, doesn't it?

'Aidan. We need to go now. Please, you have to get up and come with me to the car.'

Fay pulls on my left hand and tries to prise me off this mattress, but I'm not going anywhere. I just want to lie here and keep my eyes closed and then hopefully, I'll start to feel better soon. But Fay is persistent, annoyingly so, and she won't leave me alone.

'Get off me,' I tell her, pulling my hand back before I ask for more water.

'There's no time! We have to go!'

'What are you talking about?'

I open my eyes then to look at my wife, and when I see her face again, I notice how afraid she looks. That is the catalyst for me realising that I might not be in trouble for getting drunk, and instead, Fay might actually believe that I was drugged.

But I can't have been.

*Why would anybody drug me?*

'What happened?' I ask again as Fay has another go at pulling me up. Then she tells me, though what I hear is possibly the craziest story I've ever heard.

Apparently, I was drugged, and then Fay was taken into the basement by Bridgette and shown a woman who was tied up down there. The woman had slept with Logan, so Bridgette wanted her dead, and Fay was supposed to kill her or I would die. I stare at my wife in disbelief as she tells me that she stabbed that woman, but hopefully, she didn't die, but now we have to leave before Bridgette and Logan find out the woman might still be alive because if they do, then they will come to this barn to kill us.

I guess I'm not awake after all. I must still be dreaming or having some kind of nightmare. That's the only way any of this could make sense. But Fay is adamant that I am awake and that this is very real. Not only that, but she insists that if we don't leave now, things are only going to get worse.

I decide to trust my wife and do as she says just in case she is right, I am wrong, and this is not a dream, so I try to get up off the bed, though the process of swinging my legs over the side and putting my feet on the carpet is not an easy one.

'I do not feel good,' I say to Fay, stating the obvious but hoping my declaration will make her go a little easier on me and buy me some extra time to get myself up and moving. But Fay has no sympathy, or maybe there simply isn't time to show any, because she pulls me to my feet, possessing a strength that proves to me how afraid she is, and then she leads me to the stairs. But before we can go down them, we hear something at the bottom.

*Somebody is banging on the door of the barn.*

'No,' Fay says quietly as if she wanted to register her distress but didn't want the person outside to hear it at the same time.

'Who is it?' I ask as I reach out and hold the top of the banister for support.

'It must be Bridgette and Logan,' Fay tells me solemnly. 'They must have found out that Holly isn't dead.'

I'm not quite sure what to say to that, but it doesn't matter because Fay has walked away from me and is now over by the window, peering through the curtain to try and see who is outside. But when she does, her whole demeanour changes, and suddenly, she no longer looks afraid. Instead, she rushes past me down the stairs and seems eager to answer the door.

I still have no idea what is going on but carefully make my way down the steps to try and find out and when I get halfway down, I see Fay unlocking the door and pulling it open. But it's what happens next that is the shocking part.

*A woman covered in blood staggers into the barn and collapses in Fay's arms.*

'Help me!' Fay cries as she eases the woman to the ground, and the jolt of adrenaline I experience seems to be the thing that snaps me into action because I'm able to shake off my brain fog then and come to my wife's assistance, as well as the assistance of the woman who clearly needs our help.

As we lay her down, I see the woman's torso is soaked with blood, and some of that blood is now on the carpet, but her eyes are still open, and I can hear her breathing, so at least she is still alive. But it doesn't look like she will stay that way for long unless she gets some medical attention.

'Holly! Can you hear me? You're going to be okay!' Fay says, though I have absolutely no idea what she is basing that opinion on. Considering how far away we are from town and how we have no phone signal to call for help, I can't see this ending well for this poor woman who looks very afraid as she gasps for air beneath us.

'Stay with me, Holly,' Fay says before she turns to me and gives me a very clear instruction. 'We need to get her in the car, and we need to get her to a hospital now!'

That seems a lot easier said than done, but one thing is obvious and that is it would be good if we left this place, so I don't argue and go in search of the car keys while Fay applies pressure to the wound on the woman's abdomen. But then I hear her ask the woman where Bridgette and Logan are, but the woman struggles to answer that, so Fay just tells me to hurry up.

As I look for my keys, I hear Fay asking the woman what she should do, before I find the keys on the kitchen countertop and rush back to show my wife that I have them.

'Great, let's lift her up and get her to the car. You take the top half; I'll take the bottom!'

Fay grabs the woman's legs while I put my hands under her arms, and even though this poor person seems far too fragile to be manhandled in such a way, I realise moving her is the best chance she has of living.

As we get her to the barn door, I turn so that I will be the one to go backwards but as I do, it means I can't see where I am going. I don't think that should be too much of a problem because it's only a few yards from the barn to the car outside, but no sooner have I stepped through the doorway than I sense somebody behind me. But before I can turn to look, I feel an almighty pain across the top half of my back, and I almost drop the woman I'm holding as my eyes water, and I clench my teeth.

But that's not the worst part.

*The worst part is when I turn around and see Bridgette holding a knife.*

'Get back in!' Fay suddenly cries, having seen her too, and I don't need telling twice. We go back the way we came, and as we lower the woman to the ground, I reach out and slam the barn door shut so Bridgette can't follow us in here. Then I lunge for the handle and turn the key in the lock, and while Bridgette bangs against the door, she cannot get in.

'She stabbed me!' I say as I feel my back burning and try to gauge how bad my injury is, but when Fay checks it, she tells me it is just a slash rather than a puncture wound.

'What the hell is she doing? She's a psycho!' I cry, but Fay's face makes me realise that I am finally catching on to something she figured out well before me.

'What do we do now?' I ask my wife as she checks on the injured woman again, who is still breathing but turning very pale.

'I don't know,' Fay admits as she holds her hands over the wound and looks up at me with frightened eyes.

*That's the last thing I see before the lights go out in the barn.*

# 23

## FAY

It seems silly to think it now as I crouch here in the darkness with my wounded husband and an even more wounded woman bleeding out beside me, but there was a time when this place seemed perfect.

How times change.

Coming here was the worst thing we could have done, but it's a bit late for regrets now. We're in a fight for our lives, and considering we are trapped inside in the dark while our enemy is outside with a knife, I'd say we do not have the upper hand here at all.

I'm trying to balance helping Holly with figuring out what our next move should be, but Aidan seems to have made his mind up.

'I have to go out there and try and get that knife off her,' he tells me, but that sounds like a bad idea to me.

'No, it's too risky. She'll stab you as soon as you step through that door.'

'She's already tried once, but I wasn't prepared that time. If I can just get that knife off her, then we can get away from here.'

'No, do not go through that door,' I urge my husband, and he only has to listen to the laboured breathing of Holly lying between us to understand why I am so afraid. I don't want him to end up like this, fighting for his life on the floor while covered in blood, although I am well aware that I am the one who inflicted

Holly's injuries upon her. I guess even though she told me where to stab her and I tried my best, I still did enough damage, and while she has made it out of that basement, she hasn't made it home yet to her family.

'I need a weapon,' Aidan says, and I see his silhouette shift in the gloom, and he moves away across the barn. But my eyes are still adjusting to the darkness, so I can't see very well yet, and with a lack of moonlight outside, there is no help there either.

I keep pressure on Holly's wound and tell her again that everything is going to be okay, while internally, I am frantically trying to predict Bridgette's next move. But how can anyone predict the actions of a person like her? She's so unpredictable that I have no idea what she might try next, but one thing does seem worryingly clear. While she might have felt unable to kill Holly herself earlier, the fact she just lunged at Aidan with a knife suggests that she might have graduated from just planning a murder to actually carrying one out herself.

Something has made her mad, and I guess it's the fact that Holly is not dead after all. Or maybe it's something more.

Where is Logan?

*Has something happened to him?*

I hear Aidan in the kitchen opening drawers and cupboards, but he'll only find that the knives there are no match for the one Bridgette holds. But I doubt he'll stop looking if I tell him to, so I leave him to it and focus again on Holly, although sadly for the pair of us, it looks like I am fighting a losing battle.

Her breathing is getting much shallower now and from where I am pressing my hands into her abdomen, I can feel her pulse rate slowing. All the signs are pointing to this only ending one way for her, and as tears fill my eyes, I feel a couple of them drip onto my bloody hands below me.

'Stay with me,' I plead, but I'm not urging her loudly anymore. I'm talking more quietly now because that seems the more respectful thing to do in this woman's last few moments of life. She doesn't need to be shouted at or told what to do. Instead, she should be allowed to slip away quietly, in peace, and she should rest that way forever once she has gone. But before the inevitable end comes, I know it is important to allay Holly's biggest fear, and that's why I make sure she hears exactly what I have to say to her before she goes.

'I will make sure I find Katy and tell her that you loved her,' I say with fierce determination in my voice. 'I will find her, and I will make sure she knows that you didn't abandon her. Do you hear me, Holly? I promise you I will make sure she knows how much you cared about her, okay?'

Holly coughs then but while it's not much of an answer, I wonder if it was her best way of getting me to understand that she heard what I just said. Then, just a few seconds after I have given her my assurance, a horrible silence falls over the barn.

*Her breathing has stopped.*

'Holly? Can you hear me?' I ask, shaking her, but I already know it's over; I'm just not ready to admit it yet. I keep trying to rouse her again and again until I feel a strong hand on my shoulder, and then Aidan speaks calmly and quietly.

'She's gone,' he says, and I put one of my bloodied hands on his as I accept what he has just told me and cry heavily, all the emotion of the evening pouring out of me now.

I stay that way for a moment, not wanting to leave Holly yet because it feels so cruel to just abandon her. But I have to accept there is nothing more I can do for her at this time, and I now need to turn my focus to getting myself and my husband out of here.

'Where is she?' I say through gritted teeth as I stand up, and Aidan goes to look out of the curtain.

'I don't know. I can't see her,' he tells me, and I check out of a few more windows, but there is no sign of her through any of those either.

'Should we make a run for it?' he suggests, but I'm wary. Bridgette wouldn't just leave us, not after she knows I only pretended to kill Holly in the basement. And we still don't know where Logan is. He could be lurking out there too, with bad intentions. Unless Holly hurt him as she was getting out of the house? If so, Bridgette will definitely want revenge, so just because we can't see her, it doesn't mean we are safe.

'What should we do?' Aidan asks me, and I'm a little surprised he is putting the pressure of our next move on me. But he's aware I know our enemy better than him because while he was unconscious, I was already doing battle with her.

'I've got this,' I say as I take the corkscrew from my back pocket. 'It's not much, but maybe we can defend ourselves with it.'

Aidan takes it and gives it some thought, but it's scary to think that it may be all we have to fend Bridgette off with. She currently has so many advantages over us. She's out there in the dark; she has a knife, and while we don't know where she is, she knows exactly where we are.

How can we get to our car and drive away without her getting one good chance to stab either of us?

'We have to get out of this,' I tell Aidan as we stand together in the dark and plot our next move. 'I promised Holly that I would talk to her daughter and let her know what happened, so I have to do that. We can't die here otherwise that poor girl will never know what happened to her mother.'

'We are going to get out of this,' Aidan reassures me, putting his arms on my shoulders before bringing me in for a hug. 'I swear I won't let anything happen to you. Okay?'

I nod my head and mentally prepare myself for what I hope will ultimately be a successful escape.

'We need to get our things, though,' I say to Aidan. 'We can't leave without them.'

'I'll get the bags. You just keep watch outside,' he tells me, and as he goes upstairs, I return to the nearest window. But there's no sign of Bridgette on this side of the barn, so I go into the kitchen to try and see her out there. But while I can't see her, I do see something.

A bright orange glow a little further along the barn.

*Then I smell smoke.*

'No,' I say before running out of the kitchen to the bottom of the stairs because I need to warn Aidan. But he has already picked up on the smoke, too, because he comes down the stairs quickly, one case in each hand.

'She's set fire to the barn,' I tell him, and he nods his head before looking around.

'Let's go,' he says and heads for the door. I stay close behind him, the corkscrew in my grip. 'If you see her, shout out.'

I am willing to go along with that plan, but I'm expecting us to at least get outside the barn before we see her. However, just before we open the door, she appears on the other side of the glass with the knife raised above her head.

'Get back!' I cry, and we both retreat with the door still locked.

We were seconds away from walking out into an ambush, but now we know where she is, we know we can't go out the front way.

'The back!' Aidan cries, and he heads in that direction, but I'm not so sure that is any better because that's where the fire seems to have started, and as we enter the kitchen, we both begin to choke on the thick smoke that is growing denser by the second.

The heat is intensifying too, which tells me the fire has already taken a strong hold of this structure, but that isn't surprising because this is an all wooden building, and it will burn quickly once alight.

'I can't see anything!' I cry, and then I accidentally drop the corkscrew in my panic, losing the only weapon we had. But I don't even care about that at the moment because I'm just trying to hold onto Aidan before I lose him in the smoke and once I find him, I do not let go.

As the room gets hotter and the roaring gets louder, I fear we are going to die in here, and that fear only becomes more real when Aidan tries to open the locked back door only for him to burn his hand on the handle. I can see flames lapping at the kitchen window now and guess this whole side of the barn is ablaze.

What do we do? Try and get through the fire or go the other way, to where Bridgette is waiting with the knife?

'Aidan?' I say as the fire gets louder, and I can barely hear myself think.

That's when he turns to me and pulls me tight, and while I can't see his face through the smoke, I hear him say one thing.

'I love you.'

# 24

## BRIDGETTE

I hate to see such a beautiful building burn but needs must, and if this is the only way I can get back at Fay for the damage she has done, then so be it.

I started the fire at the back of the barn, effectively ruling that out as an escape route, and since then, I've been covering the front, just waiting for somebody inside to run out and meet a grisly end on the blade in my hand. But so far, no one has come out of the barn, and as the fire gets larger, the chances of anybody surviving inside get smaller.

The air is thick with smoke, and I have an acrid taste at the back of my throat, so I take a couple of steps back to put a little more distance between me and the blaze. I knew it would burn fast once it was alight, but I didn't think it would be this fast, and already, over half the barn is engulfed.

I think back on how long it took for a team of skilled builders to construct this place, and it's a shame to think it will be reduced to ashes in a fraction of that time. Before long, there will be nothing here but the dying embers of what once was, but it won't be the only thing that has changed around here. With Logan gone, I am now a widow, and that means life will never be the same for me again. I suspect I'll leave now, sell the house and move on to somewhere new and try to start again. I'll be fine for money, but I'm not so sure how I'll adjust to being on my own again. I'll miss Logan, flawed though he was, because while he deceived me with Holly, there are still enough good memories that we made together that will endure over time and make me look back on him with fondness.

There's a loud crack then before an almighty crash, and I suspect it was one of the support beams in the barn toppling to the floor, succumbing to the flames, just like every part of this structure will soon succumb too. But what of Fay, Aidan and Holly? I know all three are inside the barn, though in what state remains to be seen.

I followed the trail of blood from the house and all the way through the garden to the front door of the barn, so I know Holly came this way, but I'm not sure how she is doing now. She may have already died because there was an awful amount of blood, but in some ways, that may be a good thing because at least it has spared her from being trapped in a burning building. But Fay and Aidan are still very much alive and kicking or at least they were a couple of minutes ago when I saw them through the glass at the front door trying to make their escape.

I was able to scare them enough to send them scurrying back into the dark interior, and I haven't seen them since, but I know they'll be trying to get out somewhere.

*But will they succeed?*

I smirk when I think about how the back door to the cabin is locked and they don't have the key for it, so that won't be any use to them. Looking at the size of this fire now and how much smoke there is in there, I'd guess that they are unable to see their hands in front of their faces inside, so they'll struggle to look for other ways out. That's why I'm keeping my eyes on the front door, but while I keep watching, I don't see them, and the longer this goes on, the more I'm thinking they are perishing in the fire.

As the entire barn goes up in flames and the roof collapses, I know this is over, at least for Fay and Aidan anyway. But it's not over for me, and I've got a lot of tidying up to do once this fire has gone out.

As the skeleton of the barn disappears and all I see are flames, I think about how the fire has solved one problem for me but created another one. Yes, the bodies of Fay, Aidan and Holly are destroyed but the barn is too, and that means I have just lost a very nice stream of income. Renting this place out brought in some good cash, and I'd have to spend a big chunk of the profits I've made here rebuilding it if that's what I choose to do. But maybe I'll leave it. This barn was probably more trouble than it was worth and burning it to the ground might have ended up being the best thing that could have happened to it and to me. That's because while some parts of this business were legitimate, there was another side to it - a secret side that not even Logan knew about. Unbeknownst to my husband, I didn't always rent this place out to holidaymakers looking for a night away; I rented it to other people too - people who had another reason to come here.

*It was a gap in the market, and I filled it, but I only knew it existed because of my past experiences.*

As I turn and walk away from the barn, satisfied now that nobody could have survived this fire, I think about how the criminal acts I have committed tonight compare to the ones I've committed in my past. While murder was always something I thought I was incapable of, hence my reluctance to be the one who killed Holly, I've proven myself wrong there. But this is not my first time committing arson because that's a trick of mine that I've been employing since I was a teenager.

The first thing I ever set fire to was a neighbour's fence when I was ten. I'd found my grandfather's lighter and because my mum was always mad at him for smoking, I decided to go and hide it. But while I was on my way to do that, I became mesmerised when I figured out how to light the flame and once I had, I realised I had the power to create fire. I wanted to see if I could make a bigger flame. Needless to say, the fence never stood a chance.

Three more incidents of arson occurred in my teenage years, and the things I burnt ranged from a bus shelter, a skip full of cardboard boxes at the back of a supermarket and an old car that had been abandoned near my house for months. I managed to avoid trouble in the most part for those incidents because nobody knew it was me doing the burning. But it was what I set fire to when I was twenty-six that really got me noticed.

*I burnt down an entire house.*

There was nobody in it at the time, and I knew that for sure because I had watched the homeowner leave moments before, and I knew he lived alone. That man was my ex-boyfriend, and having just dumped me and broken my heart, I decided to take revenge on him and destroy his precious home. But unfortunately for me, I was caught on a neighbour's CCTV camera, and when my ex told the police he recognised me, I was swiftly arrested. The evidence meant I didn't have much of a defence, and while nobody had been physically harmed in the fire, the entire house had been destroyed, as well as part of a neighbour's property in which there had been people inside, so the judge factored that in when he sentenced me to three years.

If only I had behaved myself in prison, then I could have been out in half that time, but I found myself getting into trouble when I was behind bars. It turns out getting into fights and having banned items smuggled in only ends up adding time to a sentence, and by the time I got out, I'd been away for over six years in total.

Several years of living in awful bedsits and working low-paid, menial jobs followed, so it could hardly have been a surprise to the police when I got caught trying to steal clothes and food from a supermarket to enhance my miserable life a little. Back into prison I went, and by the time I got out again, I had absolutely nothing to look forward to besides repeating the same cycle again and again until I was an old woman.

*That was until I had the idea to befriend a man who could take care of me.*

I met Logan at a crucial time because if it hadn't been for him, I don't know what would have become of me. But he helped change my life, not that he had any true idea of what my life had been like before I met him. I just lied and gave him a fictional history, leaving out all the fires, thefts and prison time. But after moving into a big house with him and seemingly being set for life, there was one thing I couldn't leave behind.

*My tendency to play with fire.*

However, unlike in the past when I had actually played with fire, this time, the fire was of a more metaphorical kind. I missed taking risks, doing something a little naughty and pushing the boundaries a little. But not only that, I had also heard a few things during my time in prison that had given me an idea and while I hadn't thought it would come to much at the time, I realised I had the opportunity to do something about it when I saw the old barn on our new land.

Renovating the barn to be a rental holiday home was going to be 90% of the business, but there was another side to it, something else I could use the barn for that would bring in some easy but illegal money.

One thing that happens when you're in prison is that you meet all sorts of people who have committed crimes, but some of those people did not get caught straight away. Many of them went on the run before they were brought to justice, and if it had only been for a little more luck and opportunity, they could have got out of the country and disappeared overseas for good without the police ever catching up with them.

Some criminals flee to the airport, though getting caught at passport control is a big concern. Another way criminals like to try and flee the country is by getting to the coast and being either smuggled out or picked up and ferried across the sea to France, where, more often than not, they end up somewhere sunny like Spain. But it's hard to avoid the police before they can make it onto a boat, and one thing many people in prison said during our numerous chats about criminal activity was that it would be great if somebody could provide a place for those on the run to lie low before they caught that boat.

The place would have to be remote, with no phone signal or internet access so users couldn't be tracked, and it would have to be reasonably near the coast so that those who stayed could leave quickly and get out of the country when their ride was ready to take them.

It was funny, but the first time I ever saw the barn at the bottom of the garden, I just knew I had such a place.

So that was what I did. I ran a legitimate business in the most part, with nearly all my guests being law-abiding citizens, but on the side, secret to everyone but me and the criminals who stayed here, the barn was also a place those on the run could hide for a night on their way to the coast. The regular customers were treated as such, paying in bank transfers and leaving reviews on the website I had set up. But the guests who required more privacy, be it for legitimate reasons or nefarious ones, paid in cash and contacted me on a special phone number after my services had come recommended by those who had used me previously to help them evade the police.

I suppose with my history of setting fire to things, it was only inevitable that I would one day return to my favourite pastime and set this barn ablaze. But setting fire to a building is one thing. Setting fire to one when there are people inside at the time is quite another, and in this case, two of the people inside were my guests.

But which kind of guests were Fay and Aidan?

Regular ones who booked via the website because they were just a normal couple who needed a night away from everyday life?

Or two criminals on the run from the police, who paid in cash and were using the barn as a stop-off before heading to the coast to get out of England and never look back?

Well, there was a reason I asked Fay to kill Holly for me, and it wasn't because I just fancied giving her a challenge.

It was because I knew she was more than up to the task.

I knew exactly who she was, and just like her husband, she was as much of a criminal as me.

But I guess, unlike me, her luck had to run out at some point.

# 25

## FAY

I should be dead now, and maybe it would be easier if I was. But I'm still here, as is Aidan, after we escaped the burning barn, although only just.

It's been half an hour since we escaped the fiery building, but only because we got lucky. As we stood in the kitchen and tried to open the back door, desperate to avoid having to go out of the front of the house where we knew Bridgette was waiting to attack us, the kitchen window shattered, sucking out smoke and allowing precious oxygen in. But it also provided us with a way out, and Aidan quickly helped me up onto the hot countertop and pushed me through before he joined me, and together, we were able to run into the woods as the barn collapsed behind us.

I guess the intense heat in the barn caused the glass to shatter, but I'm thankful that it did because I'd hate to think what would have happened if it hadn't. I guess we would have had no choice but to take our chances with Bridgette, but while one of us might have escaped, the other one might have been gravely injured, and a 50/50 chance of either me or Aidan dying had not been something we wanted to try.

But we've both made it away from that crazy woman, although our problems are far from over. That's because we're both lost in the woods without our car, meaning travelling is going to be tricky now. We managed to get our most prized possessions out of the barn too in the form of our wallets, purses and ID's, but anything else would only slow us down more, so we had to leave our suitcases full of clothes. But at least we're both alive and not only that, but Bridgette will think we are dead, meaning we would have the upper hand if we were to go back and get revenge on her, which is something that I am very keen to do.

*But Aidan does not agree.*

'Let's keep going and get as far away from her as possible,' he tells me, eager for us to forge on through the woods rather than go back and try to make Bridgette pay for what she did to us.

'Are you kidding? We can't let her get away with this!' I cry, my voice loud in the quiet woods, but there's nobody else around, other than my husband, to hear me. 'She tried to burn us alive! She drugged you! And she made me stab a poor woman to death! I'm going back there, and I'm going to kill her!'

I turn to go back in the direction of the barn, although it's so dark out here, and we ran so fast to get away initially that I have absolutely no idea which way I would have to go to get back there now. But even before I can try and make a start, Aidan grabs my wrist and stops me from going anywhere.

'Leave it, Fay! It's too risky! We almost died, but we got away. Why can't you just be grateful for that?'

'Grateful? What have I got to be grateful for?'

'We're still alive,' Aidan tells me. 'And that's all that matters. We're still here, and we can still make our plan work. But we have to go now otherwise we won't have time. We can't waste it going back. We just need to keep moving.'

Aidan's reference to our plan is almost laughable, given all that has happened since we made it, and I'm not sure how he can seriously think we can just try and carry on as normal when things are anything but.

'We have to go back. We can't let her get away with this,' I try once more, but Aidan refuses to let go of me.

'She thinks we're dead, and let her think that. She hasn't won; we have! Can't you see that?'

It doesn't feel like a victory at all, but Aidan is adamant we are not going back there, and as I calm down a little more, I realise what he is telling me is right. We should not go back; we should just try and stick to our plan. But how can we do that?

'What do we do?' I ask him, feeling almost as helpless as I did back in that basement and in the burning barn. 'We haven't got a car. We'll never get to the meeting point in time without it.'

'There's a road near here,' Aidan says, gesturing ahead. 'I heard cars when I went for my walk earlier. If we can find it, we can try and get one to stop.'

'What? That's too risky. What if the driver recognises us and calls the police? Or what if a police car drives past and sees us by the side of the road? Or what if he sees all this blood on me and freaks out?'

My fear of being arrested is almost as strong as the fear I felt when I was surrounded by flames because as far as I'm concerned, I could not survive in prison, which means I'll do anything to avoid it.

'Take off your blouse,' Aidan tells me, obviously because that's the item of my clothing that has the most blood on it.

'What? No, it's cold!'

'You can wear my jacket. Just zip it up,' he says, taking off his jacket and urging me to hurry up and do as he says.

I comply, tossing away my blood-stained blouse in exchange for his jacket before Aidan goes on.

'We have no choice but to try and hitch a ride with someone. We can't walk to the meeting point, can we?' Aidan cries, growing frustrated with me, but I'm entitled to debate our next move with him rather than just follow him head-first into a mistake.

'It's too risky!'

'And going back to the barn isn't?'

'But we might be able to steal Bridgette's car and drive that to the meeting point,' I suggest, rather hopefully.

'Or we might get stabbed or burnt or have something else horrible happen to us because that woman is a psycho and is far too dangerous to be around.'

I know in my heart that Aidan is right, and going back is not a good idea, but the thought of putting our complete faith in some passing driver on the road up ahead seems just as ludicrous. But Aidan urges me to follow him, and without wanting us to get separated, I have no choice.

We move on through the eerily quiet woods, and despite what Aidan said about hearing cars around here earlier, I sure can't hear any now. But ten minutes and a whole lot of internal worrying later, we break through the tree line to see a road cutting through the fields in the distance. But because it's the middle of the night, the road is devoid of cars.

'Come on, we have to try,' Aidan tells me, and we move on, heading for the road and hoping that somebody will come along it soon, somebody who might be able to help us get out of here and to where we need to be much sooner.

But we're so far from our initial plan now that I can't help but grow more anxious the closer we get to the road. This was not what was supposed to happen when we came here. The idea was for Aidan and me to disappear from view for twenty-four hours before driving on to meet the person who was going to help us get out of the country. That's why the barn was perfect. Nobody would know we were there, least of all the police officers who were looking for us at home. But now we are giving them a chance to catch up with us before we can get out of England and into mainland Europe, and I hate that fact, though there is little I can do to change it.

'If our photos are in the news now, do you think the driver might recognise us?' I ask Aidan as we walk on towards the road.

'No,' he replies, feigning confidence. 'That's why we changed our appearance. My beard, your hair colour; it'll still work. We look different to the photos the police will issue and soon, we'll be gone.'

I can only hope that my husband is right as we hurry across what is most likely a farmer's field, though even this hour of the day is too early for any farmer to be awake. I have to take confidence in my new red hair that has replaced the blonde hair I used to have, making me look different enough to not be noticeable when my photo is soon all over the front pages of British newspapers. Aidan with his beard and glasses, now looks different from his clean-cut demeanour of old, which should make it just as hard for somebody to recognise him from his photos too. But that still doesn't mean I'm going to enjoy tempting fate.

It was bad enough stopping off at the service station on the way down here to get fuel and supplies because it meant showing our faces in a public area. But that felt manageable as long as we avoided eye contact with anyone, moved quickly and also stayed apart, making it less obvious we were a couple. But now we're talking about getting into somebody else's car, meaning it will be impossible to look at them, go unnoticed and pretend we're not together; therefore, increasing the odds our identities might be exposed later down the line. Aidan doesn't have his baseball cap with him like he had at the service station either, so that's another thing not in our favour as we reach a small fence and climb over it before heading through the last field that separates us from the road.

As we move across the wet grass, its surface slick with the dew that won't dry until the sun comes up several hours from now, I think about how Bridgette was the only person who knew who we were when we came to Kent. She knew the truth because I was honest with her, and that's how she knew we were on the run from the police. That's why we went to her, and that was why she took us in.

I guess it was also why she figured I would be able to kill Holly for her.

*Because I told her I'd already killed before.*

To be fair to her, Bridgette did not seem shocked when I explained to her what I'd done and why. She promised me she would be very discreet, and after telling me how much cash she required for her services, I told her we would be with her soon, as early as possible, if that was okay.

And it was.

But just because the journalists in the newspapers will soon be writing about me doing something terrible, it doesn't mean any person who reads those articles will know the real me. It'll just be one version of me, one very heavily edited and heavily biased version, and there is so much more to my story - far more than a journalist or any random member of the public could assume. Not only them, but my family and friends too, the people I have left behind and accepted I will never get to see again. They don't really know what has happened to me, what I have been through and why I have done the things I've done, just like they don't know those things about Aidan either. That's why the pair of us have to stick together.

*We're the only ones who really know each other.*

But there is one thing about me that Aidan doesn't know, although I'm sure he will one day soon.

He doesn't know that I am a killer. As far as he knows, I'm just running with him because of the crimes he's committed.

*Not the ones I'm guilty of too.*

'There!' Aidan says as he suddenly points ahead, and when I look up, I see a set of headlights glowing in the distance. But they're not just glowing, they are moving towards us, and as Aidan breaks into a sprint, I start running with him too.

'Wait! What are we going to say if they stop?' I ask Aidan, but he doesn't answer as he increases his speed and makes it to the roadside before waving his arms in the air and attempting to attract the attention of the approaching vehicle.

I have no idea what the driver is going to make of seeing such a sight at this time of the morning, just like I have no idea if they are going to actually stop and let us in their car. But Aidan is certainly trying his best to make them hit the brakes, and unbelievably, the driver actually seems to be doing that because the vehicle slows as it gets nearer, no doubt because Aidan is now standing in the middle of the road right in front of it.

As the vehicle stops and the male driver stares out of his windscreen at the pair of crazy people who almost got run over trying to get his attention, I hold a hand up to my face to shield my eyes from the brightness of the headlights. But there's another reason I am putting my hand over my face.

It's because I'm trying to reduce the chances of this driver recognising us and calling 999 because for all I know, the true extent of our crimes have been unearthed back home since we have been in Kent, and our photos could be all over the internet for anyone to look at.

Are they?

If so, will our disguises work?

*Or is this driver going to be the one who finally brings a stop to my and Aidan's supposedly perfect escape?*

# 26

## FAY

### *BEFORE THE ESCAPE*

'I don't understand. What do you mean all the money has gone?'

I stare at Aidan in disbelief, waiting for his answer, which I am praying will be one good enough to alleviate all my fears and show me that this is not the disaster I think it is. But Aidan does absolutely nothing to calm me down, not even saying a word. All he does is reach for the bottle of wine I had been saving for a dinner date with friends this weekend, and after he unscrews the lid, he doesn't even bother getting a glass out of the cupboard.

He just drinks straight from the bottle.

*Yes, this must be as bad as I feared.*

'Aidan, talk to me!' I cry, rushing towards him and attempting to take the bottle from his hand. But he turns away from me and keeps the bottle within his grasp, and that seems very important to him. It's only when he finally speaks again that I understand just why he needs a strong dosage of alcohol at this time.

'I've done something stupid,' he says quietly before taking another swig. 'I thought I was being clever, but I've been an idiot, and I'm really sorry, I am, but I think we're screwed now.'

'*We're* screwed?'

Aidan nods his head before going for another gulp. I didn't realise it was possible to drink wine so fast.

'Aidan, talk to me. What have you done?'

I'm trying to piece together exactly how my life could have suddenly fallen apart when five minutes ago, I was standing in this kitchen looking at the menu for our local takeaway and deciding what to order. But a moment later, Aidan came in, and I could tell that something was wrong as soon as I saw him because all of the colour had drained out of his face, and he did not look at all like a man who was eagerly anticipating ordering his own tasty meal soon.

*He looked more like a man who was being forced into ordering his last meal on Death Row.*

Aidan slumps down into one of the chairs at the kitchen table, still nursing the bottle of wine, though he refrains from taking another drink for long enough to give me a little more information about his predicament.

'I've been taking money out of the company,' he says, his voice as meek as a naughty schoolboy sitting in the headmaster's office. 'More money than I should have been. It wasn't mine to take.'

'What are you talking about? It's our company.'

'Yes, but it wasn't profit,' Aidan says before looking up at me sheepishly. 'We've been losing money for the last two years, not making it.'

I frown because that does not make any sense.

'What? I've seen the accounts, and I've helped sign off on the figures. We're doing well. I mean, I know you mentioned there had been a bit of a downturn over the last couple of months due to the markets fluctuating and affecting supplier prices, and things weren't as good as they were, but I thought we were still doing okay. I thought overall, business is good.'

Aidan laughs then before chugging from that damn bottle again.

'Business is good,' he repeats, quoting me and still chuckling, but I'm not finding any of this funny and to prove it, I lunge forward and swipe the bottle from his hand, causing it to fly against the wall and shatter.

'Hey!' Aidan cries as he looks at the mess I have just made, but I turn his cheek so he is facing me again because that's the only place his attention needs to be.

'Aidan, what are you talking about? What is going on with the business?'

And that's when my husband and business partner tells me everything. How the business we started together was growing in the early days but nowhere near quick enough for his liking, so he decided to start cutting a few corners. Claiming expenses that weren't really expenses. Burying some profits so he wouldn't have to pay tax on them. He kept this secret from me because I only had a passing look at the accounts on a semi-regular basis, unlike him, who oversaw them all, along with the accounts assistant, Lana, who I know all too well from what had happened with her earlier. She has since been let go from our company - one of my non-negotiable requests after I found out she had more than a professional relationship with my husband - but it seems by then, much of the damage was already done.

Aidan then tells me how he went further in his bid to make the company seem like it was doing better than it was and began chasing more money, eager for the fast cars and sharp suits he had dreamt of as a youngster. That was when he started producing fraudulent invoices and tax returns, and as he funnelled money out of the company, the records belonging to that company became more fictitious by the day.

I am stunned to hear all of this because I had absolutely no idea any of this was going on. As far as I was concerned, we were doing well barring the one issue with a big client going bust and being unable to pay us, and while we were a few years away from early retirement yet, I believed we were in a very secure place financially. But according to Aidan, just like with his brief fling with Lana, it was all built on a bed of lies.

And then he gives me the worst part of it all, the part that had got him so worked up that he had started drinking from the bottle.

'Lana is going to go to the police,' he tells me solemnly. 'She's mad at us for firing her, so she's going to tell them everything. Then they're going to investigate, and they're going to have all the evidence they need. I'm screwed, Fay. And the company is too.'

*Which means I am.*

'Please tell me you're joking,' I say as I sit down opposite Aidan and put my head in my hands. 'Please tell me this is just some practical joke.'

'It's not. I just got a text from Lana telling me she hates me and will be speaking to the police and will make her allegations. They'll come and arrest me then and shut everything down until they have looked into it all.'

'We have staff! Employees who have homes and kids! What will happen to them?'

'I don't know,' Aidan says as he buries his head in his hands too. 'I wasn't thinking properly.'

'Damn right, you weren't! You were just thinking about having a flashier car and more expensive holidays! How could you have been so stupid? And how could I have been so stupid not to know what you were doing?'

'This isn't your fault,' Aidan tells me as if that is supposed to make me feel any better.

'Damn right, it isn't my fault; it's yours! But it's my mess now because I'm stuck in this with you. I'm your wife, and it's my name alongside yours as a director, so I'm just as culpable as you in all of this, whatever this is. Financial crime. Fraud. Tax evasion. Anything else?'

'I'll tell them you didn't know anything about it. I'll say it was all me.'

'It was all you! Well, you and that woman you cheated on me with!'

I hate Lana even more than I already did as I realise something.

'If she was helping you do this, you must have been giving her money to keep quiet about it, right?' I ask. 'How much did you give her? How much was she taking from our company without me knowing?'

Aidan looks like he does not want to answer that, but as I think about how Lana always had new nails, new dresses and a sparkly silver watch that can't have been cheap, I

realise not only was she sleeping with my husband for a while, she was being paid off by him too.
I could strangle that woman if she was here now, just like I am seriously tempted to strangle my husband at this table. But then I have another thought.

'Wait a minute. If she's going to the police about what she helped you do with the accounts, won't she be in trouble as well?'

That might be one silver lining to this whole nightmare because I sure wouldn't mind her going to prison for her sins. But Aidan disappoints me yet again when he tells me that as a lowly accounts assistant, she could just say she was pressured into doing it by her manager, and the fact she has confessed and exposed this will go in her favour too. Sure, it's unlikely she'll ever work in an accounts department again, and she might get a suspended sentence, but she won't bear the brunt of the law.

*That will be left for my husband and possibly me too.*

'We're going to lose everything,' I realise. 'The business. The house. The cars. Everything. All because you got greedy.'

There is a rage bubbling up inside of me, and I'm going to have to unleash it somewhere. When I do, me smashing that bottle of wine against the wall is going to look feeble in comparison. But as I look at where the wine hit the wall and see the dark red liquid dripping down onto the tiled floor, I wonder if there might be a way out of this mess, at least as far as the police are concerned anyway.

'Wait, you said Lana hasn't gone to the police yet, right?' I say, and Aidan nods, though he doesn't appear to be on my wavelength yet or else he might start to get a little more colour back in his cheeks.

'Well,' I go on. 'Maybe we can stop her. Change her mind.'

'Why would she do that for us?' Aidan asks.

'I don't know. We'll pay her. Buy her silence. Do anything to stop her from making this any worse. We have to try something!'

'It won't work.'

'How do you know that?'

'Because I've already tried!'

I stare at Aidan and realise this must have been going on for a while now if he is admitting to already having tried to pay Lana to keep her silence.

'You tried to bribe her?' I ask, amazed so much could have been going on behind my back.

'Yes, but she doesn't want money. She just wants to see me suffer, and you, too. She wanted me and because she can't have me, she hates you. You fired her, and I stopped replying to her messages, so as far as she is concerned, she wants to see us pay, big time.'

Aidan seems to think this is well past the point of retrieval, but I'm not going to just sit here and wait for our lives to fall into complete ruin without at least knowing I tried my best to prevent it.

'We have to go and see her, and we have to get her to change her mind,' I say. 'And we have to do it now.'

'No, it's too late,' Aidan says, shaking his head. 'She told me that if I come near her again, then she'll have me arrested for harassment on top of all the other charges that will be coming my way soon. I can't go anywhere near her.'

That sounded like a clear threat, and realising Aidan going to see Lana would only make things worse, I dropped the idea of us both going to see her. But something had to be done, and as Aidan went to sleep that night, I stayed up, plotting our next move.

Before I knew it, I was in my car and driving to Lana's house after finding her address still saved in our historic employee intranet system, and as I arrived, I was hoping this whole unsavoury situation would somehow have a happy ending.

*Unfortunately for Aidan and me, going to Lana's house that night was the worst possible thing I could have done.*

# 27

## FAY

*PRESENT DAY*

Cars. Humans rely on them so much, don't they? We need them to get us around. From Point A to Point B. We'd be totally lost without them and unable to get anywhere fast. But cars cause problems too, though I'm not just talking about traffic accidents and pollution. I'm talking about how cars have the ability to take us humans to places we shouldn't go.

A car took me to Lana's that fateful night.

*Because it did, I've been having to use cars ever since to try and get away.*

Aidan's car got us as far as the barn, but after things went so disastrously there, we needed another set of wheels, and thanks to the driver who pulled over by the side of the road, we have them. My husband and I are sitting in the back of a vehicle that is unfamiliar to us and being driven by a man who is just as unfamiliar to us.

But this is no taxi, nor is it a pleasant journey.

I'm constantly on edge as I glance nervously at the eyes of the man in the rear-view mirror and wonder if he is making the link between his new passengers and any possible news story that might have leaked in the last several hours. I guess not so far because he hasn't stopped driving yet and told us to get out, nor has he taken us to the nearest police station. For the time being, we seem to be going exactly where he told us he would take us, which is Folkestone, a town on the southeast coast that is not exactly where we need to be but is not far off. That's where the driver was going when he stopped for us, and we're extremely grateful for his help, so we aren't going to grumble and ask him to take us all the way to Sandgate, the village we ultimately need to get to. We can walk there from Folkestone and as well as that, it's better if this driver does not know our final destination.

*That way, he can't tell the police should he ever be questioned at a later date.*

'It's been a while since I did any camping myself,' our driver, a chirpy man in his fifties by the name of Derek, tells us. 'I used to quite enjoy it as a child, but it seemed to lose its appeal as I got older.'

The reason Derek is talking about camping is because of the cover story Aidan and I gave to him just before he allowed us into his car. Aware that we needed a good reason as to why we were wandering around in the middle of nowhere outside of daylight hours, Aidan told him that we had got the train here from up north and been camping in the woods nearby, but our tent had collapsed and being unable to fix it, we had given up and decided to try and get some help to get out of here. It was a fanciful tale, but we leaned heavily on being two city-dwelling northerners who were down south on holiday and were simply a little out of our depth and because of that, he took pity on us. When he told us he was going to Folkestone, we said that was perfect and we quickly got in, not wanting to risk him changing his mind and driving away, leaving us stranded by the roadside again.

Derek had chuckled to himself as we climbed into his back seat, no doubt amused that we had got ourselves into a bit of bother, but the main thing was that he believed our story, and as he has driven us on, everything seems to be going okay. We're getting closer to the place we need to be at, although we aren't due there for a while yet. But things have changed and with the need to put more distance between us, the barn and Bridgette, we are having to adapt.

But before I can spend any more time thinking about that woman and how I still have unfinished business with her as far as I'm concerned, Derek says we are here and asks us where we would like to be dropped at. I presume he thinks we'll be looking for a hotel, but the problem is neither Aidan nor I know the names of any hotels here. Fortunately, I spot the neon glow of the sign for a 24/7 supermarket, so I tell Derek that leaving us there will be great.

'I need some snacks and a strong drink after tonight,' I tell the driver and while he laughs because he thinks I'm traumatised after a camping mishap, I am just glad he has no idea what I am actually traumatised about.

'Thank you so much,' Aidan says to the driver after we have both got out of the car.

'No worries. Maybe be more careful next time,' Derek says before giving us a friendly wave and driving away, leaving the pair of us standing in the middle of the chilly and mostly empty supermarket car park.

'That seemed to go okay,' Aidan observes as we watch Derek's headlights disappear into the distance, but I guess neither of us can be too sure about that. For all we know, Derek just acted like he didn't know who we were and is now racing to Folkestone police station to tell the officers on duty there that he just picked up a couple of hitchhikers who he suspects are actually on the run. With that in mind, we better not linger around here for too long.

'That sign says it's two miles to Sandgate,' Aidan says, pointing to the road sign that is visible beneath the glowing streetlamp. 'That's about a forty-minute walk.'

'Let's get going then,' I suggest, and we do just that, although we have to be cautious because without any mobile phones to help us, we have to rely on old-fashioned signs rather than hi-tech maps that show us precisely where we are at any given moment.

'How long have we got?' I ask Aidan as we leave the supermarket car park, neither one of us wanting to try our luck by going inside to get a drink and ending up being caught on camera.

'Three hours,' comes the reply, and we quicken our pace then without conferring with each other on that.

As we make our way through a deserted Folkestone, I can hear the sound of the tide nearby, and as well as smelling the salty sea air and hearing a couple of seagulls cawing overhead, I know we are right on the tip of the southeast coast now. But we're not quite at the exact point on this coastline we need to be, though we should be soon.

*That's the point where the boat will pick us up and take us to France.*

The original plan for Aidan and I had been for us to leave Bridgette's cabin before dawn and make the short drive down to this part of the coastline before boarding a boat and leaving England behind for good. That hasn't quite happened like that but we're here now and that's the important thing, meaning we can finally return our focus to exactly what needs to happen for this perfect escape of ours to actually succeed.

I've never spent much time at sea before, and the closest I ever usually get to such a large body of water is whenever I've been sunbathing on the beach. I've never fancied going on a cruise, and I'd much rather fly over water than sail across it. But all that is about to change shortly because Aidan and I have quite the journey ahead of us.

The motorboat that will pick us up to make the illegal voyage will be small, unsheltered and operated by a man who has already received half of the fee he requested to make such a voyage. The second half will be payable when he gets us to our destination, or that should be *if* he gets us to our destination. There are no guarantees that he will be able to get us safely out of England without either the coastguards catching us or the boat encountering difficulties and sinking. It's a clear, calm night, so that is a huge help, but that also means it might be easier for any police boats that patrol this coast to see us as well. They'll be out looking for all manner of people, from drug smugglers to migrants, and while it's a vast sea and a huge area to cover, not everybody slips through undetected. Some boats get stopped and even if they don't, they might sink well before returning to land.

Soon, drowning in freezing water will be just as much of a fear as ending up in handcuffs, but it's a risk we're going to have to take if we want to get out of England because one thing is for sure.

We can't stay here.

But the driver of the boat will be just as worried about getting caught or drowning as we are, so I expect him to take all the necessary precautions and get us to France, from where we will then move on as quickly and as quietly as we can in the direction of Spain.

*And then the idea is to start a new life under false identities.*

Can we do it? Will we really get away with what we've done? Is there a chance we won't have to pay for our crimes?

I guess time will tell.

For now, we'll just keep on walking as the seagulls fly overhead and the gentle waves roll in and out, as unobstructed and relentless as the paranoid thoughts have been in my mind ever since that fateful night at Lana's house.

# 28

## FAY

### *BEFORE THE GETAWAY*

It's past ten o'clock in the evening when I park outside Lana's house, but I don't care that it's late or that she might be getting ready to go to bed. I'll kick her front door down to get in if I have to, and the way I feel as I get out of the car, I'm almost hoping I get the chance to.

As I prepare to knock on her door, I'm fully aware of what is at stake here. Either I can convince Lana not to go to the police and report Aidan or she will carry on as she currently plans to and ensure that all of my husband's crimes within our business are fully exposed and laid bare for a judge to mull over. Then, he'll be in custody, and I'll either be on the outside, alone with all my bank accounts frozen, or I'll be sitting in a prison cell as well.

After knocking, it takes a minute before the door is unlocked and opened and when it is, I see Lana standing before me in a light and flowy nightdress, the kind she can get away with wearing when she has a body like hers. I can see why Aidan was charmed by her, but then again, he was charmed long before he saw her wearing something as casual as this. From what I gathered, all it took for their brief fling to start was her giving him a lot of attention and a couple of dazzling smiles, and his mind was running riot with the possibilities. Who knows how long the affair would have gone on for if I hadn't caught them together at the office one night? It might still be underway to this day but if it was, Aidan's financial crimes would still be secret too. As it is, everything is out in the open now, as open as the front door I stand on the doorstep of.

'What are you doing here?' Lana asks, stunned to see me paying her a visit, as well she might be.

'We need to talk,' I say calmly but forcefully, but Lana is just as forceful when she tries to slam the door in my face. Fortunately, I'd already been prepared for that and put out my hand to stop the door before it could fully close. Then, using all the frustration I have inside me from tonight's events so far, I push as hard as I can, and the door flies back open, sending Lana stumbling back into her hallway.

'What are you doing?' Lana cries, but I ignore her as I step into the house before I reiterate my desire to talk.

Lana is much more mild-mannered now than she was a moment ago when she tried to slam the door shut, and she backs down for a moment and tells me to do just that then.

*Talk.*

'Look, I know you have a grievance with me and my husband over how you left the company,' I say, beginning gently. 'But Aidan has just told me what you are doing, and it is serious. Aidan could go to prison for a very long time if you talk to the police. Is that really what you want? Him inside, locked up with dangerous criminals? I get that he broke your heart, but guess what?

He broke mine too. But that doesn't mean I want him arrested, and you don't want that either, right?'

'Who are you to tell me what I want?' Lana asks, not responding in the manner I'd hoped. 'You have no right to come here and tell me what I should and shouldn't do. You lost that right when you made me redundant, even though we all know the only reason you got rid of me is because I slept with your husband!'

'That may be so, but come on, Lana. Don't be stupid. From what Aidan has told me, you'd be in just as much trouble as him if the police really started digging around. So just drop it. If you do that, we are willing to give you something. Something to make up for all of this.'

'What makes you think you can bribe me? Aidan already tried that,' Lana says, still not talking the way I hoped she would, especially now I've just played my trump card, which was the offer of something to make this all go away. Okay, it's a bribe, but it's also money to a woman who has just lost her job, so shouldn't she be more grateful, or at least a little more receptive, to the idea?

*It seems not because now, Lana is telling me to get out again.*

'Please, Lana,' I say. 'I know I've made mistakes, but it's not just Aidan who might get in trouble here. The police might implicate me too, even though I didn't know anything about what Aidan was doing with the finances. I don't deserve to go to prison. Don't do this to me. Aidan already broke my heart, and now I've just found out that he's been doing illegal things with our business. I've suffered enough too, but if you carry on, not only will I lose my husband, I'll probably lose my home too.'

It's a desperate, last-ditch attempt to change Lana's mind, but will it work? A woman as scorned as her has vengeance on her mind, so she won't care about who gets hurt along the way, especially not when she knows I was happy to see her leave the company.

*Unfortunately, I am right.*

'You've got ten seconds to get out of my house, or I'm calling the police, and they'll add trespassing and attempted bribery to your husband's list of crimes,' Lana says ominously, and I don't doubt that she will do that for one minute. But I can't give up this easily.

'Name your price,' I say desperately. 'How much would it take for you to not talk to the police?'

Lana looks surprised that I've just essentially handed over a blank cheque. But at least I have her attention again, and she isn't telling me to get out anymore. Instead, she appears to be thinking about that number I just asked her for.

'A million pounds,' she says a few seconds later, though when I hear that figure, I almost burst out laughing.

'We don't have that much to give you,' I say, and it should be obvious to Lana that I'm telling the truth because while the business was doing quite well, or so I thought, it was not a seven-figure one.

'Too bad, that's my price. Never mind!' Lana says with a shrug and a smirk, and I realise then that she just picked some outrageous number to show that she

really means it when she says she doesn't want money. She has no intention of being paid off.
*She really does want her revenge.*

I gulp then when I realise it really is impossible to buy her silence.

'Oh dear,' Lana says when she has seen my face drop. 'Doesn't feel good to be so powerless, does it? Now you know how I felt when you fired me.'

'Wait!' I try, hoping I can buy some time. 'Just be sensible here. Us going to prison won't make your life better but money will, and we have some. It's not much, but we can get it for you. I have a couple of thousand pounds in an account. I can get you the cash when the banks open tomorrow.'

'Wow,' Lana says, looking surprised. 'After all your husband has done to you, you're willing to give me all your money to keep him safe.'

'It's not about him,' I insist. 'It's about me and all the other innocent employees who don't deserve to be tarnished with his brush. You two were the ones in on this crime, not anyone else, but if you go to the police, everyone at the company will fall under suspicion, and that's not fair.'

'Too bad because a couple of thousand pounds is nowhere near enough to stop me talking. I gave you my figure, and you can't match it, so get out, or I will call the police now and get them here tonight!'

To prove her point, Lana grabs her phone from the hallway table then and appears to be making a call. As far as I know, she is dialling 999, and that's why I panic and rush towards her, desperate to get that phone out of her hand before she can do any more damage to us.

I reach for the mobile, but she keeps it away from me, and in my frustration, I push her. Lana looks a little fearful then because she can clearly see in my face how desperate I am here, and I guess it makes her realise I might be willing to go much further than she first thought to get her to keep quiet. But it seems she already has a back-up plan for that, just in case.

'What are you going to do?' she asks me as she tries to keep her distance from me. 'Hurt me? If that's what you're thinking, then just know that it won't help you. I've already told a friend about what Aidan has been doing, so if anything happens to me, she'll tell the police, and they'll know to look at your husband.'

'You've done what?' I cry, terrified that this secret extends beyond the three of us.

'That's right, bitch. Someone else knows. So you're screwed whatever happens next!'

Lana takes satisfaction in making that point, but even though she might be right, I cannot let her feel like she has got another victory against me, not after she has already slept with my husband.

*That's why I rush towards her and let all my anger and frustration out in one quick move.*

I push her backwards as hard as I can, with no thought for her wellbeing, just a deep desire to see that smile wiped off her face. Maybe it was also my desperation not to have the police come here and arrest me for trespassing and intimidation tonight but whatever it was, I pushed Lana as hard as I could, and it was a relief when I saw her drop her phone before a call had connected. But it was not so much of a relief when I saw her fall back and hit her head on the stairs, and after hearing a loud crack, I felt sick at the sight of her neck appearing to now be in a very unnatural position.

I stood frozen in fear and shock as I waited for Lana to open her eyes and stand up, but it didn't happen. She was not moving and, by the looks of it, not even breathing.

Then I realised I could either stay and call her an ambulance and explain this to them.

Or I could run.

*So I ran.*

# 29

## FAY

### *PRESENT DAY*

It's difficult to find a specific meeting point along a coastline in the middle of the night. But it's even more difficult when you're sleep deprived and anxious, the latter being the minimum consequences that come from killing a person and trying to get away with it.

I never meant to kill Lana, or at least that's what I've been telling myself ever since I pushed her and watched her bang her head on the stairs. But she died, although I did not hang around to call the emergency services for her and see if there might have been anything they could have done to save her. I just left her house as quickly as I could, went back home and then made a plan.

*And this is the end result of that plan.*

'I think this is it,' Aidan says when he spots the yellow ribbon tied to the fencepost along the coastline in Sandgate, a small village that is like a ghost town at this time of night.

I think my husband is right because we were told to look out for a yellow ribbon, and now we've found it, we know the boat that is due to come and pick us up will be coming to this point.

I wonder how many other people have stood here before us and waited for their illegal passage out of England. Perhaps we're the first on this section of the beach because it would surely be a good idea if the ribbon moved around, just like it would be a good idea if the boat did not take the exact same route every time. But this operation must be successful enough to keep going because we're definitely not the first people to try it, although as we stand on the beach and stare out at the quiet, calm sea, I worry that tonight, the operation will have been exposed by the coastguard and the boat will have been seized by the authorities. If it has, it will not be coming to pick us up. Either the police will be coming or we will be left standing here uselessly, stuck in this country and out of options.

While Aidan has enough to worry about with the laws he broke with our business, I have the fear of going to prison for murder to drive me to get out of here. I have no idea exactly how many years I would be sentenced to if I was put on trial, but even if I was only found guilty of manslaughter, it would be a long time before I was free again. I'd be far closer to fifty than forty by the time I was out again, that's for sure, but even being found guilty of manslaughter might be optimistic. I had a clear motive to want to hurt Lana, and any prosecutor would look to exploit that to give me the harshest possible punishment. They would say that I went to Lana's house that night to kill her, and based on all the reasons I had to hate her, I don't think any jury would have a hard time agreeing with them. Even I would be inclined to agree with them because, if I'm really honest, what happened with Lana was not an accident.

I was afraid, and I was desperate, but I knew what I was doing when I pushed her over. Okay, so I expected her to get up again when she fell, but even if she had got back to her feet, I was hardly going to just walk away from her then. I'd had enough of her ruining my life, and even though she warned me about her friend knowing about Aidan and his crimes, I didn't care at that point.

I just wanted her to respect me, and if that wasn't working, the next best thing was to shut her up.

But because that friend did know, a friend I had no idea how to find, I knew Aidan nor I would ever get away with this. My husband would be the prime suspect when her body was found, and even if I confessed to save him from going on trial for a crime he didn't commit, what would my defence be? Could a lawyer be skilled enough to paint a picture to the jury of me being a woman who was just acting in self-defence or out of a necessity to protect her employees at the business - people who did not deserve to lose their jobs if the police shut down the office? They could make out that Lana was threatening us, and I got scared, and while some of that is true, she did not for one second try to put her hands on me. That means she was not a threat in the physical sense.

I made the first move.

I attacked her first.

*To say anything else in court would be a lie.*

That is why I would rather not put myself in that position. I want to avoid all courtrooms if I can, just like I want to avoid a police cell or interrogation room. Why leave my future to chance and put my fate in the hands of other people when I can try and control it myself?

That's why, after I had gone home and tried to figure out what to do next, I knew there was only one course of action I wanted to take.

*I wanted to run.*

As I stand here shivering on the beach and look out to sea, in hope more than expectation, I know that just getting this far was not guaranteed, even after I had decided to try and get away with what I'd done. It's one thing to want to leave your life behind and just disappear, but it's another thing to actually pull it off, so even after I'd decided to make a getaway, there was still a lot I had to figure out if we were going to make it work.

*The first thing was convincing Aidan that running was the right thing to do.*

That was easier said than done because while my husband was aware of the severity of his crimes, he had no idea I had done something even worse than him. He wasn't aware that I had gone to Lana's house that evening, and he certainly wasn't aware that I had ended up killing her.

I made a decision when I got home that night not to tell Aidan what I had done. I simply couldn't trust what his reaction would be. At best, he would be shocked to the point of not being able to do much of anything of use, and that would be no good. At worst, he would panic and go to the police, possibly afraid that they would try and pin the murder on him if they didn't suspect me.

I knew I had some time because Lana lived alone, so with a bit of luck, her body wouldn't be discovered for a few days. But the longer I left it, the more I knew her friend would worry and when she did call the police, the risk of them coming to our front door would increase. Even if they were more interested in talking to Aidan at that point, I couldn't bear the thought of having to be around them because I just knew I'd panic in their presence and give myself away. That's why the next morning, after Aidan had woken up and I had endured a sleepless night, I told him what I felt we should do.

'Let's go. Let's just leave,' I said, as if it was as simple as that, though I knew from what research I had done that night after killing Lana that just abandoning one's life and starting a new one elsewhere was difficult, if not almost impossible.

'What are you talking about?' Aidan had said, stunned at my suggestion.

'I don't want you to go to prison, and I don't want to stay here if we can't be together, so let's go. We could pack our things and just get in the car and drive. We've got time before the police come here, so we could be far away by then. We could get into Europe, Spain, maybe. Change our appearance and our names and just start afresh. Wouldn't you like that?'

While many people might quite like the idea of just starting again somewhere new, very few people actually do it, and Aidan could scarcely believe I was suggesting it for us. But I kept telling him it was the only way for us to stay together, and while I sold him on it all being about saving him from trouble, I knew secretly that it was as much about me getting away with something too.

When he said he might consider it, I still had a lot of convincing to do, but I'd been up all night thinking about how it might work, so I ran him through my thoughts.

So much of my planning in that initial stage was based on things I had seen in television shows and films rather than based on any real-life experience I might have had, and that was why the first thing I had decided we needed to do was not just leave our home, but leave the country. But quite quickly, I realised there was one big problem with that. Even if we did make it to the airport and get on a flight, there would be a record of that, and it would be pretty clear to the police where we went. I only had to read a couple of real-life news stories online about people who had either been stopped at passport control or arrested in the country they had landed in to scare me off flying away.

It seemed the best way to get away with what we had done in the long term and disappear completely was to do exactly that.

*Disappear.*

That's why I decided to try and think of alternative ways to get out of the country.

But what does a person new to crime know about being smuggled out of the country?

The answer to that question was absolutely nothing at first, but with more research, I discovered there were places on the internet one could go if they were seeking certain illegal things, one of them being safe passage out of the country without detection by the authorities.

Using my laptop that I planned to destroy once I'd finished looking at numerous nefarious websites, I descended deeper and deeper into the dark web, a murky part of the internet where criminals roam freely, and it was there I learnt many interesting things that could help us. I found a man on a chatroom forum talking about how he had gotten out of England twelve years ago and could help anybody else who needed to do the same, and as I read his account, it became clear going down to the south coast was our best route to take. But he also mentioned that depending on when we could be transported out, we would need a place to lay low for a while as close to the pick-up point as possible, and that was how I found out about Bridgette's barn house.

Advertised as somewhere in a remote region near the coast with no internet access or phone signal, it sounded like the perfect place for us to hide out, so after I had found somebody who could pick us up by boat, a person I hoped was a real smuggler and not an undercover police officer, I also looked at booking a night at the barn, offering to pay in cash, of course, so there was no trail.

I told Aidan what we could do if he was willing to give it a go, and while it took me almost all the next day to convince him, he eventually said yes. I think the tipping point was me spending half an hour showing him stories of other people's experiences in prison - experiences that terrified him and, indeed, me in equal measure.

With him agreed, I said we had to change our appearance, so while I bought hair dye, Aidan went and bought a pair of glasses and a baseball cap and decided to hold off on shaving his already two-day-old stubble. Then we packed as lightly as we could and emptied our bank accounts of as much cash as we could before getting into our car and driving away from our house.

It was a very quickly conceived plan but one that could work if we stuck to the rules I'd read online. But several things have gone wrong along the way, not least of which was Bridgette turning out to be a crazy person, but while at the time I just thought we had been unlucky with her turning out to be crazy, the more I think about it, the more I suspect she actually knew who we really were.

While Lana's death and our possible connection to it had not hit the news when we left home, I wonder if it had by the time we were staying in Bridgette's barn. How else could she have known that I was capable of killing Holly for her? She had to have known what either Aidan or I had done.

*If so, why would she kill the woman she had tied up in the basement when there was already a killer staying at her barn?*

It's ridiculous, but I burst out laughing then, not because I'm actually amused by what's happened, but because I simply can't comprehend the absurdity of it all. If being so unfortunate as to marry a man who cheated on me and broke the law wasn't enough, I ended up killing a woman after simply pushing her over before

I then booked a night's stay with a psycho who knew who I really was and what I was running from.

'What's funny?' Aidan asks me as my laughter breaks the silence on this quiet beach.

'Everything,' I say, still chuckling. 'All of it. None of it. It's just mad, isn't it?'

Aidan looks troubled by my slightly maniacal reaction to our desperate situation, but chooses to say nothing and we spend a very long time then in silence. Minutes turn to hours with the pair of us barely saying another word to the other until suddenly, we both hear something out at sea.

*It's the sound of a motorboat engine.*

'It's him,' I say, and we set off towards the water, waving our hands above our heads to attract the attention of the man in the boat.

It's at that point I wonder if the person coming to pick us up is an undercover police officer and this is where our daring and crazy escape ends. It sure would fit right into all the bad luck I've had so far. But as the boat stops a few metres from shore and the man encourages the pair of us to wade out to him, I see no sign of a police identification, nor are there any helicopters swarming overhead or vans parking on the road behind me and unleashing their trained canines to stop us getting any further.

All is quiet - almost too quiet - but as Aidan rolls up his trousers and enters the water, I realise this is really happening.

We're getting out of England.

We're getting away with what we have done.

But we're not the only ones, and once we're safely in the boat and heading out to sea, I think about Bridgette again.

I can't forget her and what she put us through.

*Just like I'm sure she can't forget us.*

# 30

## BRIDGETTE

It's been two weeks since the barn burnt down and everyone inside it died. In that time, I've started the clean-up operation the best I can, trying not to think too much about how much of the ashes and embers that I have been scooping into bin bags might contain the remains of those who died in the fire. In that time, I've had a chance to reflect on all that occurred, and while I am glad I ultimately won, I am aware that I caused a lot of the trouble myself, and so many things could have been avoided if only I had done things differently.

I recognised Fay and Aidan when they arrived here and I took them the cake, even though they had clearly gone to some lengths to change their appearance. Already aware that a couple were coming to stay with me because they needed a place to lie low, something Fay expressed very clearly after telling me that she had seen I came recommended in certain ways, I knew they were running from something. Usually, I don't like to busy myself with finding out what any potential criminal clients might have done before they come here because that's none of my business. I just make sure I give them somewhere they can stay until they move on and, ideally, disappear. But in this case, with a woman in my basement and revenge on my mind, I was curious. It might have turned out that the crimes they were running from were not of the kind that could be of any use to me,

but I thought I should try and find out just in case. And I'm glad I did, or at least I was at the time.
After putting their names in to a search engine, I found a few articles on the Yorkshire news in which they were mentioned. Apparently, the police wished to speak to the married pair, not only over allegations made about their business, but, more interestingly, in connection with the discovery of a woman's body at her home.
Were they killers?
*If so, maybe I had somebody to do my dirty work for me in terms of Holly.*
Because the full story hadn't unravelled yet, it wasn't making national news, which is why Logan hadn't heard about it, and therefore, he was never going to have a chance to recognise them. But because I already had some inkling, I not only saw through their attempts at a disguise, but knew they could possibly help me, so I made my plan.
Drug Aidan because it would be easier to deal with an angry woman than an angry man, and then put that woman to the test. I knew that if she was running with her husband, then she was clearly desperate to stay with him; otherwise, she might have run alone. Therefore, I knew there was a good chance she wouldn't allow me to hurt her partner and leave that basement without doing what I'd asked.
But while I used my knowledge of Fay's past to my advantage, I perhaps should not have tempted fate. I could have just dealt with Holly myself and left Fay and Aidan alone and if I'd done that, they would be alive now, and the barn would still be standing and available

for somebody else to hire. Alas, that is not the case, and as I look at my phone and see another email in my inbox from somebody hoping to hire the barn for a short stay, I am now forced into telling them the barn is unavailable and will no longer be an option in this area for the foreseeable future.

There goes a good income stream.

*But it's not the only thing I've lost.*

After leaving the burnt-out barn, I went back to the house and used the landline phone to call for an ambulance to come and help my husband, whom I said I had found lying downstairs after I had woken up in the early hours of the morning and realised he hadn't come to bed himself. When the paramedics arrived, I acted like a woman who had just got the shock of her life would - crying, asking questions and simply telling the emergency workers that they had to save him. But all they did was grimly confirm what I already knew.

Logan was gone. He had not survived what appeared to be a heart attack, and after his body had been taken away, an examination confirmed the cause of death. But with the seemingly innocent way in which he had passed, combined with his medical history of high blood pressure, the police had no questions for me surrounding what might have caused his heart attack, and that was that.

It was handy having the barnhouse out of sight from the cottage because none of the emergency workers there that night saw that there had been a fire and even when one of them mentioned the smell of smoke in the air, I just told him that youths were always burning things in the fields around my place at night.

While I miss my husband and wish he was still around, I am learning to live without him, even though it is awfully lonely here in this place now he's no longer here. I know I should move, and I will, and nobody will think it is weird because many widows change their address after losing their partner, seeking a change of scene so they can try and move on without being surrounded by constant reminders of what has been lost. But while I will get around to putting this house up for sale, I am still here for the time being and trying to enjoy my home the best I can. The tastefully decorated interior. The peace and quiet. And the space - the room I have to move here being far more than what I had when I was in those prison cells not so long ago.

As I'm just preparing to spend another quiet day by myself, a day in which I will reflect further on everything that has gone on in the past while also making a few more plans for the future, I hear a knock at the front door.

When I answer it, I find a smiling man on my doorstep.

But that's not all I discover because he has a gun, and he is pointing it right at me.

*That's the last thing I see before he pulls the trigger.*

# EPILOGUE

## FAY

The sky is blue, and there is not a cloud in the sky as I gaze out across the Mediterranean Sea and smile to myself. We did it. We got away. The police in England have no idea where we are, and as long as we can continue to lay low here with our new identities, they never will.

How does it feel to get away with murder?

*Pretty damn good, though it's not just Lana's murder I am guilty of anymore.*

As I watch a small speedboat cutting through the clear blue sea in the distance, I think about the journey that helped us get here to sunny Spain. It was a cold, wet and very windy boat ride to the north of France, only made entertaining by how much I was thinking about Bridgette and how I had to make her pay for what she had done to us and Holly. Delicious thoughts of revenge had been ripe in my mind as we had sped across the sea, and by the time we were travelling through France on our way south into Spain, I'd already decided that she had to die.

I just didn't know how at that time.

*But I soon figured it out.*

Stepping away from the sun-kissed balcony I've been standing on, I make my way back to the table inside the restaurant where Aidan is waiting for me. He has a menu in his hands and a glass of red wine in front of him, and he smiles when he sees me retake my seat opposite him.

'How's the view?' he asks me as I pick up my own menu.

'Beautiful,' I tell him.

'My view is just as good,' he replies with a cheeky wink, and I roll my eyes at his cheesy compliment before I begin perusing all the food options at this fish restaurant that has quickly become our favourite since we arrived in this town and figured it was a good place to start a new life.

Money was an issue when we first got here, mainly because any funds we had in bank accounts back in England had been frozen, and we'd spent half of the cash we had taken from the ATM on paying Bridgette and the boat driver. We converted the last few hundred pounds we had into euros and used that on a booking at the cheapest hotel we could find, but at that point, going out for expensive meals seemed a million miles away. Fortunately, with our new identities already paid for before we left England, we were able to find work quite quickly.

I've been working in a clothing factory, which is boring, tedious work, but thanks to my ability to speak English and some broken Spanish from my school days, I have progressed from a lowly worker on the factory floor to helping process some overseas invoices in the admin team. The pay isn't too bad, and the location of the factory helps give me a very low profile - things that are very different to when I commanded a big salary as the co-director of a successful business back home.

Meanwhile, Aidan has been helping out with the accounts at a local business, although he has been under strict instructions to stick to the rules this time and not get creative with the numbers again because that's what got us into this mess in the first place. But the money we have started bringing in means we can soon rent our own place, and it will be a relief to get out of the basic, bedbug-ridden hotel.

For now, this meal at this fancy restaurant is a treat to remind us that we can still enjoy a few of the finer things in life, even though our lives are very different now and can never be what they once were.

'I'll have the shellfish,' I say to the pleasant waiter with the impossibly perfect suntan, before Aidan orders the lobster, and then we clink our glasses together to toast to a lovely meal to come.

After we have done that, I can't help but glance nervously around the restaurant because one of the things I simply have no choice but to get used to now is the fact that I'm always going to be on edge and looking over my shoulder. All it would take is for one person to recognise either of us, and the police would be in here and slapping handcuffs on our wrists before marching us away from all the seafood and the wine and that beautiful view from the balcony. Such is life on the run, I suppose. It can't all be sunshine and sea views. I'm never going to be able to truly relax, though it's a small price to pay to avoid prison.

But the chances of somebody recognising us here are small. Most of the people here are Spanish, so they won't be paying much attention to what is going on in the British newspapers. The main issue is the sizeable ex-pat community over here, namely all those who are British and have left to move to sunnier shores here. There is far more chance of them recognising us from the photos that have made their way into the newspapers, although that fades every day because along with our new look, we also have a deep tan now, making us look even less recognisable from the pale faces in the photos back home. We've also been careful to use accents, speaking in a dialect that is identifiable from a different part of the country to where we originated, not to mention spending time apart, so people don't always know we are a couple. As far as my work colleagues know, I am single, just like Aidan's colleagues think he is too, so that makes it even harder for somebody to figure out we are that married couple that the police in England cannot find anywhere. When we do go out together, we only go to places like this, where locals go, not tourists, which makes us blend in even more.

'Relax, it's fine,' Aidan says to me when he notices me looking around the restaurant to see if anybody is looking back at us.

I nod my head and take another sip of wine and start to unwind a little more, my back and neck sore from my last shift at the factory but my taste buds tingling in anticipation for my meal to come.

'I was thinking,' Aidan says as he smooths out his napkin on his lap. 'Once we've got settled in our own place and a little more time has passed, we could look at starting our own business.'

'I hope you're joking,' I reply, and to my utter relief, Aidan tells me that he is.

'Got you,' he says with a smirk before reaching for his wine. 'Even I'm not that stupid to make the same mistake twice.'

I roll my eyes and let Aidan chuckle away to himself but while he's easily amused, I still have things on my mind that make it much more difficult for me to laugh. The main one is that I miss my family and friends terribly and hate the fact that I can't reach out to them and let them know where I am or what I am doing. The media are saying such horrible things about us and without being there to give my side of the story, I fear all my loved ones must hate my guts now.

If they don't hate me for the crimes Aidan and I have been accused of, then they will surely hate me for just leaving without saying a single word to them, but that was just how it had to be. They would have tried to talk me out of leaving and even if they hadn't, they could have passed on information to the police that might have seen them catch us quicker. As it was, we were out of the country before anybody even knew we had fled, and that's the only reason we're sitting in this restaurant now instead of a prison cell.

One thing that is no longer occupying my restless mind is Holly and her daughter, Katy. After giving that dying woman my word that I would reach out and tell her estranged child that she had not willingly left her like she had done the last time, I did my research and tried to learn more about Holly online in the hope it would lead me to her daughter. But all it actually did was tell me that Holly was on the run herself after attacking and almost killing an ex-partner of hers. She was not a regular customer at that barn, but a criminal looking to lie low like me and as for her daughter, she didn't even exist. Holly had spun me a lie, obviously to try and have me take pity on her so I wouldn't take her life after Bridgette demanded it, and I fell for it.

Does that make me feel any better about delivering the blow that ultimately took her life?

*Actually, it does.*

'Here we go,' Aidan says as he rubs his hands together, and when I turn around, I see our waiter carrying two plates piled high with delicious seafood right to our table. I smile as our plates are set down in front of us before thanking the waiter, using a little of the Spanish I have already picked up since I've been here. It's not much, but it's nice to make an effort, and, in a year or so, I aim to be fluent, which would certainly go even further towards helping me keep my cover here.

But while I am technically on the run here because of the crimes the police already suspect us of, there is one crime I have gotten away with that nobody knows I had any involvement in.

*And that is Bridgette's murder.*

As I tuck into my meal, I think about how my very fast and very steep descent into the criminal underworld led me to paying a man I was meeting in a Spanish bar late one night to do me a favour. Having used the internet to find a way to get out of the country, I'd also been able to more recently use it to look into the

idea of hiring a hitman to carry out one very specific job for me.
Finding it impossible to allow Bridgette to go on thinking both that we were dead and she had won, I contacted a man over the internet and enquired about whether or not he fancied paying a visit to that house in the remote region of Kent. Once the meeting was arranged and money had exchanged hands - money I kept secret from Aidan by telling him the boat over had cost more than originally planned - I was to await evidence of the crime being committed.

The photos I was shown three days later were proof that Bridgette had died on her doorstep, but in the end, I hadn't even needed to wait for those. That's because the assassination of a woman in her home in a place as peaceful as the Kent countryside had made the national news, meaning I knew for sure that she was dead well before I saw the graphic images to prove it.

With her gone, I do feel a little bit better about how everything ended at the barn, though I still wish Holly had survived and I could have been the one to give Bridgette her comeuppance personally. But what's done is done, and it was money well spent. What's more, Aidan has no idea that I was behind arranging Bridgette's murder. He just presumes she had other enemies, and that seems likely considering what she had proven herself capable of. But I'm glad he doesn't know it was me, though not just because there is no need for him to.

*It's also because I don't want him to have any idea of what is going to happen to him soon.*

As I savour my shellfish and sip my wine, I smile to myself, and when Aidan notices how happy I am, he asks me what I'm thinking about. But I don't tell him the truth, just like he didn't tell me the truth about the business or Lana until his hand was forced. Instead, I just keep smiling before telling him that I'm glad we were able to get away.

He smiles when he hears that, and why wouldn't he? But he wouldn't be smiling if he knew what I was really happy about. He wouldn't be smiling if he knew that very soon, once I've saved up some more money, I will be making another request to that hitman I hired to kill Bridgette, and this time, I will be sending him to see my husband.

You didn't really think I was going to let him get away with what he did to me, did you?

He was the one who started this whole unimaginable time in my life.

It's only right that I am going to be the one to end things.

*For him, anyway.*

As for me, I hope to have many more happy years ahead of me in the Spanish sun, and over time, I'm sure all thoughts of England will fade into the background, and one day I'll learn to stop stressing and worrying so much.

We all deserve the chance to escape from it all, right?

*THE END*

## Download My Free Book

*If you would like to receive a FREE copy of my psychological thriller 'Just One Second', then you can find the link to the book at my website www.danielhurstbooks.com*

Thank you for reading *The Perfect Escape.*

If you have enjoyed this psychological thriller, then you'll be pleased to know that I have several more stories in this genre, and you can find a list of my titles on the next page. These include my most popular book *Til Death Do Us Part*, which has a twist that very few people have been able to predict, and *The Doctor's Wife*, which became the #1 selling book in the UK Kindle Store in February 2023.

# ALSO BY DANIEL HURST

TIL DEATH DO US PART
THE PASSENGER
WE USED TO LIVE HERE
THE DOCTOR'S WIFE
MY DAUGHTER'S BOYFRIEND
THE INTRUDER
WHAT MY FAMILY SAW
THE HOLIDAY HOME
THE BRIDE TO BE
HER LAST HOUR
RUN AWAY WITH ME
THE RIVALS
WE TELL NO ONE
THE WOMAN AT THE DOOR
HE WAS A LIAR
THE BROKEN VOWS
THE WRONG WOMAN
NO TIME TO BE ALONE
THE TUTOR
THE NEIGHBOURS
THE BREAK
THE ROLE MODEL
THE BOYFRIEND
THE PROMOTION
THE NEW FRIENDS
THE ACCIDENT

*(All books available now on Amazon and Kindle Unlimited – read on to learn a little more about selected titles…)*

# TIL DEATH DO US PART

***What if your husband was your worst enemy?***

Megan thinks that she has the perfect husband and the perfect life. Craig works all day so that she doesn't have to, leaving her free to relax in their beautiful and secluded country home. But when she starts to long for friends and purpose again, Megan applies for a job in London, much to her husband's disappointment. She thinks he is upset because she is unhappy. But she has no idea.

When Megan secretly attends an interview and meets a recruiter for a drink, Craig decides it is time to act. Locking her away in their home, Megan realises that her husband never had her best interests at heart. Worse, they didn't meet by accident. Craig has been planning it all from the start.

As Megan is kept shut away from the world with only somebody else's diary for company, she starts to uncover the lies, the secrets, and the fact that she isn't actually Craig's first wife after all...

# THE PASSENGER

***She takes the same train every day. But this is a journey she will never forget…***

Amanda is a hardworking single mum, focused on her job and her daughter, Louise. But it's also time she did something for herself, and after saving for years, she is now close to quitting her dreary 9-5 and following her dream.

But then, on her usual commute home from London to Brighton, she meets a charming stranger – a man who seems to know everything about her. Then he delivers an ultimatum. She needs to give him the code to her safe where she keeps her savings before they reach Brighton – or she will never see Louise again.

Amanda is horrified, but while she knows the threat is real, she can't give him the code. That's because the safe contains something other than her money. It holds a secret. *A secret so terrible it will destroy both her's and her daughter's life if it ever gets out...*

# THE WRONG WOMAN

***What if you were the perfect person to get revenge?***

Simone used to be the woman other women would use if they suspected their partner was cheating. She would investigate, find out the truth and if the men were guilty, exact revenge in one form or another. But after things went wrong with one particular couple, Simone was forced to go into hiding to evade the law.

Having assumed a new identity, Simone is now Mary, a mild-mannered woman who doesn't raise her voice or get angry, meaning nobody would ever suspect her of being capable of the things she used to do for a living. But when she finds out that her new boyfriend is having an affair, it awakens in her the person she used to be. Plotting revenge, Mary reverts back to the woman she once was before she went on the run and became domesticated. That means Simone is back, and it also means that her boyfriend and his mistress are in for the shock of their lives.

**They messed with her. *But they picked the wrong woman.***

# THE WOMAN AT THE DOOR

**It was a perfect Saturday night. *Until she knocked on the door...***

Rebecca and Sam are happily married and enjoying a typical Saturday night until a knock at the door changes everything. There's a woman outside, and she has something to say. Something that will change the happy couple's relationship forever...

With their marriage thrown into turmoil, Rebecca no longer knows who to trust, while Sam is determined to find out who that woman was and why she came to their house. But the problem is that he doesn't know who she is and why she has targeted them.

Desperate to save his marriage, Sam is willing to do anything to find the truth, even if it means breaking the law. But as time goes by and things only seem to get worse, it looks like he could lose Rebecca forever.

# THE NEIGHBOURS

**It seemed like the perfect house on the perfect street. *Until they met the neighbours...***

Happily married couple, Katie and Sean, have plenty to look forward to as they move into their new home and plan for the future. But then they meet two of their new neighbours, and everything on their quiet street suddenly doesn't seem as desirable as it did before.

Having been warned about the other neighbours and their adulterous and criminal ways, Katie and Sean realise that they are going to have to be on their guard if they want to make their time here a happy one.

But some of the other neighbours seem so nice, and that's why they choose to ignore the warning and get friendly with the rest of the people on the street. *And that is why their marriage will never be the same again...*

# THE TUTOR

## *What if you invited danger into your home?*

Amy is a loving wife and mother to her husband, Nick, and her two children, Michael and Bella. It's that dedication to her family that causes her to seek help for her teenage son when it becomes apparent that he is going to fail his end of school exams.

Enlisting the help of a professional tutor, Amy is certain that she is doing the best thing for her son and, indeed, her family. But when she discovers that there is more to this tutor than meets the eye, it is already too late.

With the rest of her family enamoured by the tutor, Amy is the only one who can see that there is something not quite right about her. But as the tutor becomes more involved in Amy's family, it's not just the present that is threatened. Secrets from the past are exposed too, and by the time everything is out in the open, Amy isn't just worried about her son and his exams anymore. She is worried for the survival of her entire family.

# HE WAS A LIAR

***What if you never really knew the man you loved?***

Sarah is in a loving relationship with Paul, a seemingly perfect man who she is hoping to marry and start a family with one day, until his sudden death sends her into a world of pain.

Trying to come to terms with her loss, Sarah finds comfort in going through some of Paul's old things, including his laptop and his emails. But after finding something troubling, Sarah begins to learn things about Paul that she never knew before, and it turns out he wasn't as perfect as she thought. But as she unravels more about his secretive past, she ends up not only learning things that break her heart, but things that the police will be interested to know too.

Sarah can't believe what she has discovered. But it's only when she keeps digging that she realises it's not just her late boyfriend's secrets that are contained on the laptop. Other people's secrets are too, and they aren't dead, which means they will do anything to protect them.

# RUN AWAY WITH ME

***What if your partner was wanted by the police?***

Laura is feeling content with her life. She is married, she has a good home, and she is due to give birth to her first child any day now. But her perfect world is shattered when her husband comes home flustered and afraid. He's made a terrible mistake. He's done a bad thing. *And now the police are going to be looking for him.*

There's only one way out of this. He wants to run. *But he won't go without his wife...*

Laura knows it is wrong. She knows they should stay and face the music. But she doesn't want to lose her man. She can't raise this baby alone. *So she agrees to go with him.* But life on the run is stressful and unpredictable, and as time goes by, Laura worries she has made a terrible mistake. They should never have ran. But it's too late for that now. Her life is ruined. The only question is: *how will it end?*

# THE ROLE MODEL

***She raised her. Now she must help her…***

Heather is a single mum who has always done what's best for her daughter, Chloe. From childhood up to the age of seventeen, Chloe has been no trouble. That is until one night when she calls her mother with some shocking news. There's been an accident. *And now there's a dead body…*

As always, Heather puts her daughter's safety before all else, but this might be one time when she goes too far. Instead of calling the emergency services, Heather hides the body, saving her daughter from police interviews and public outcry.

But as she well knows, everything she does has an impact on her child's behaviour, and as time goes on and the pair struggle to keep their sordid secret hidden, Heather begins to think that she hasn't been such a good mum after all. *In fact, she might have been the worst role model ever…*

# THE BROKEN VOWS

***He broke his word to her. Now she wants revenge…***

Alison is happily married to Graham, or at least she is until she finds out that he has been cheating on her. Graham has broken the vows he made on his wedding day. How could he do it? It takes Alison a while to figure it out, but at least she has time on her side. *Only that is where she is wrong.*

A devastating diagnosis means the clock is ticking down on her life now, and if she wants revenge on her cheating partner, then she is going to have to act fast. Alison does just that, implementing a dangerous and deadly plan, and it's one that will have far reaching consequences for several people, including her clueless husband.

# WE USED TO LIVE HERE

***How much do you know about your house?***

When the Burgess family move into their 'forever' home, it seems like they are set for many happy years together at their new address. Steph and Grant, along with their two children, Charlie and Amelia, settle into their new surroundings quickly. But then they receive a visit from a couple who claim to have lived in their house before and wish to have a look around for old time's sake. They seem pleasant and plausible, so Steph invites them in. And that's when things start to change…

It's not long after the peculiar visit when the homeowners start to find evidence of the past all around their new home as they redecorate. But it's the discovery of a hidden wall containing several troubling messages that really sends Steph into a spin, and after digging deeper into the history of the house a little more, she learns it is connected to a shocking crime from the past. *A crime that still remains unsolved...*

***Every house has secrets. But some don't stay buried forever…***

# THE 20 MINUTES SERIES

What readers are saying:

*"If you like people watching, then you will love these books!"*

*"The psychological insight was fascinating, the stories were absorbing and the characters were 3D. I absolutely loved it."*

*"The books in this series are an incredibly easy read, you become invested in the lives of the characters so easily, and I am eager to know more and more. Roll on the next book."*

THE 20 MINUTES SERIES (in order)

**20 MINUTES ON THE TUBE**
**20 MINUTES LATER**
**20 MINUTES IN THE PARK**
**20 MINUTES ON HOLIDAY**
**20 MINUTES BY THE THAMES**
**20 MINUTES AT HALLOWEEN**
**20 MINUTES AROUND THE BONFIRE**
**20 MINUTES BEFORE CHRISTMAS**
**20 MINUTES OF VALENTINE'S DAY**
**20 MINUTES TO CHANGE A LIFE**
**20 MINUTES IN LAS VEGAS**
**20 MINUTES IN THE DESERT**

**20 MINUTES ON THE ROAD**
**20 MINUTES BEFORE THE WEDDING**
**20 MINUTES IN COURT**
**20 MINUTES BEHIND BARS**
**20 MINUTES TO MIDNIGHT**
**20 MINUTES BEFORE TAKE OFF**
**20 MINUTES IN THE AIR**
**20 MINUTES UNTIL IT'S OVER**

# About The Author

Daniel Hurst lives in the Northwest of England with his wife, Harriet, and daughter, Penny, and if that doesn't make him lucky enough, he considers himself extremely fortunate to be able to write stories every day for his readers.

You can visit him at his online home www.danielhurstbooks.com

You can connect with Daniel on Facebook at www.facebook.com/danielhurstbooks or on Instagram at www.instagram.com/danielhurstbooks

He is always happy to receive emails from readers at daniel@danielhurstbooks.com and replies to every single one.

Thank you for reading.

**Daniel**

THE PERFECT ESCAPE by Daniel Hurst published by Daniel Hurst Books Limited, The Coach House, 31 View Road, Rainhill, Merseyside, L35 0LF



Front Cover Design by 100Covers

Printed in Great Britain
by Amazon

28607965R00142